WED TO THE LICH

Arranged Monster Mates

Layla Fae

CONTENTS

CONTENT WARNING

T here are two major content warnings for this book: eating disorder and body dysmorphia. If that is triggering to you, this book might not be the best pick as it's not just one scene or chapter but a recurring theme throughout the story.

A complementary trigger: memories of verbal abuse by a guardian.

Another content warning to be considered: an evocative description of animal death in chapter 15.

If you'd like to know more details, see below, but be advised they contain spoilers.

SPOILER
SPOILER
SPOILER

SPOILER

The heroine has been intentionally starved and brainwashed by her guardian and displays physical and psychological symptoms of advanced anorexia nervosa.

The animal that's killed is a fawn.

PROLOGUE

No one remembers the world before the Shift. It was thousands of years ago, all lost, all forgotten. Scientists and historians say that before, the world was better, brighter, and our planet belonged to us, humans. There were proud countries and bustling cities, and technology was at its highest.

We can hardly imagine all that. There is no proof, no written texts, no pictures of Alia Terra before the Shift. All we know is the face of Alia Terra now. The land haphazardly divided into territories, the walled cities, the poor living on the fringes, barely surviving.

The monsters.

The temples where young virgins can take a DNA test and be matched to one of them. An arranged marriage to a monster is often the only way a woman can save herself or give her family a chance to not starve.

This is Alia Terra. It belongs to the monsters, and

we belong to them.

CHAPTER 1

Virgil

"Thank you."

I kept my voice quiet and low, and yet, the priestess startled, her eyes darting to my face and away just as quickly. She gathered the paperwork clumsily, making the paper rustle. Her hands shook.

"T-that's all," she said, coming out from behind the marble counter and stopping a distance away from me. Without looking up, she said, "F-follow me, s-sir. She's... She's waiting."

Instead of setting out toward our destination, the priestess froze suddenly. Her face colored, her mouth twisting to the side. I cataloged her features, noting the crease between her eyebrows, the blush, the tension around her eyes and jaw. It seemed to me she was upset.

"Maybe you should reconsider!" she blurted out, her eyes darting to my face. "She's only nineteen, too young to be married."

The priestess didn't look at me for long. They never did. And as soon as she beheld my face, the upset emotion drained out of her, replaced by a disgust and horror she couldn't quite hide.

At least, I thought it was that. Human expressions were never easy to read for me, but those two were familiar and expected. I knew what horror looked like in every race I ever encountered. It didn't make me feel any emotions, but then, hardly anything did these days.

I watched the priestess in silence, focusing on what she said while she shook, waiting. Would I reconsider? Should I?

Maybe if I left now, it would be for the best. Maybe forcing a hapless human to look at my face every day would be cruel. I did not know, because even though I took the temple's course, I still knew almost nothing about Alia Terra's humans. Was fear very unpleasant? Did it hurt them?

If it did, maybe I should leave, after all. Before it was too late.

But then I thought about Aurelius. About Makwa, Quirilian, Zuriel. All my neighbors and friends who chose eternal sleep and would never be again. I thought how lonely they were before they went away, one by one, extinguishing the lights in their eyes, letting their beautiful homes fall into disrepair.

My race was dying a slow death. It was quite ironic, but it was also tragic, and since my flame still burned strong, it was my duty to keep our line from extinction.

Besides, was it really evil, what I was trying to do? I looked to my left where an enormous male troll stood, towering over the priestess who checked his paperwork. She smiled, which meant she was friendly toward him, and they talked pleasantly.

"She will be very happy to have you," caught my ear.

I looked at the priestess responsible for my case, her sickly skin clammy with terrified sweat, and I wondered.

Why would a human bride be happy to have a troll, but not a lich? I paid the required sum that was supposed to support her family. I took classes at the temple to learn everything I needed about her handling and care. I would cherish her and give her everything she required.

Why shouldn't I have a bride?

It was the loneliness in me speaking, I knew. Liches were supposed to be lonely, our species solitary by necessity. Our feeding grounds had to be substantial, so we lived spread apart, visiting rarely. But sometimes, at one or two points in his life, a lich felt a craving for... companionship.

That was the word I used when filling out my questionnaire. But it was more than that. So much more.

I felt it, stirring in my chest, a cool sensation sliding against my ribs, like a sound barely heard, a song of longing and pain. And I knew if I didn't heed it, I would do what my neighbors did. I would lie down in my mausoleum and sleep until all energy dripped out of me.

And then I would not feed. My body would harden as the last sparks left it, and then... I would be gone.

My bones would crumble and turn to dust, and while my soul would still hover in the place of my eternal rest, asleep and at peace, I would be no more.

I needed her. Without my bride, I'd be gone.

"I considered the matter very carefully," I told the priestess, keeping my voice as human-like as I could for her comfort. "And I'd like to meet my bride now."

She opened her mouth as if to say something and then shook her head, pursing her lips, and turned. She walked fast, and I followed her, looking around curiously. When I caught the troll's eye, his expression shifted—*horror, disgust*—and he looked away.

I might think it was rude if I didn't know that reaction was natural and instinctive to all living organisms. They were alive, I wasn't, and that caused them profound discomfort.

Maybe the fact I could drain the life out of whoever I laid my eyes on was another cause for fear. But I hadn't done it in centuries. And I'd never drain a troll. Their life energy looked very unsavory.

I brightened, remembering how I once told that to a troll female who was paralyzed by fear when she saw me. I wanted to put her at ease, so I told her I didn't feed on trolls because I didn't like the smell.

For an unfathomable reason, she was offended.

I stopped trying to put living creatures at ease some time after that. It wasn't worth the effort, and it never worked.

But I would have to try with my bride, wouldn't I?

The priestess led me down a wide corridor with walls and floor of beautifully veined blue marble, lit with torches. I glanced at the dancing flames, the fire's energy calling to me, and I had a sudden urge to devour it.

Just one.

Fire would make me warmer. It would make me seem alive, and maybe then, I wouldn't scare my bride too violently.

I really shouldn't feed in public where people could see it. If they were terrified just looking at my face, seeing me devour something, even if it was just fire, would send them into a panic.

And yet... I felt so tempted. I really wanted to make a good first impression.

My bride was the only person I didn't want to fear me.

I gave in and looked behind me, picking a torch. I felt for the fire's crackling energy and let the tendrils of my shadow unveil, racing. They were barely visible, and if the priestess looked back, she'd see moving shadows teeming with a glittering darkness.

She did not, of course, look back. My shadow reached the torch and wrapped around it lovingly, drinking all the powerful heat and energy out of the fire until it extinguished, the torch not just snuffed out, but cold as if it was never lit at all.

My eyes dimmed as the hot, thundering crackle of the flames flowed into me. Everything inside me thrummed, and I faltered, my steps unbalanced. The world brightened around me, coloring with the fire I just consumed.

It grew golden, bright warmth suffusing my vision, and I stared around in wonder as shimmery, golden pleasure filled my body.

Damn it, I thought, shaking my head to clear it when the priestess stopped by a tall, golden door and waited for me to catch up.

I hadn't fed in a long time, and now, the heat and energy was much too potent. When I was starved, taking in something so powerful and yet insubstantial went straight to my head.

Like alcohol for humans, I thought in a daze, remembering the course I took. *It makes one unstable.*

So we were similar in one way, at least: we shouldn't consume our pleasures on empty stomachs.

But there's another similarity, my unbound mind supplied, the thought slipping through the cracks of my control. *The way humans and liches mate is practically the same. Barring a few minor differences.*

I shook my head again, the loud buzzing in my bones feeling dangerously like hunger. With difficulty, I bound my shadow to me, and yet small tendrils slipped free, dancing around me and sampling the air.

As I neared the priestess, they reached out to her, and I tensed, calling on all my control. I couldn't feed off this woman. I could not feed off humans, period.

If I did, she would shrivel up, years of life sucked out of her, and if I didn't stop in time, she would drop dead on the floor. And I would be barred from the temple.

They would never give me my bride if I did that.

More determined than I'd been in a long time, I wrestled with my hungry nature, binding it close to me so it could not touch anyone. I worked fast, the heat of the fire slowly dissipating out of my bones, my grip strengthening.

When the priestess opened the door, motioning inside with a trembling hand, I had myself under control.

"I'll be back in a m-minute," she said and left, not waiting for me to step inside.

Slowly, pressing the mantle of my shadow close to me in case it got out of control again, I walked inside the wedding chamber. It was gloomy, just a bright blue fire burning ahead of me, keeping the corners of the room dark.

I heard a small gasp and sensed rather than saw her first.

A luminous, delicate energy, like that of a flower or a moth, glittered in a faint cloud in the darkest nook. In my heightened state, it called to me like something delicious and forbidden. Like a beauty so perfect, one has the urge to smash it. Like something so fine, one can't help but want to possess it, completely and utterly.

Mine.

Undone by sensing something so extraordinary, my defenses fell, and I opened myself fully to experience her in all her glory. Her energy undulated with her every breath. I heard the susurration of blood in her veins, the rustle of her clothing, the sharp nervousness of her breathing.

I perceived all of her before I even saw her, and everything in me readied, instincts taking over.

There she is. My bride.

I turned my eyes on her, making them shine a light to penetrate the gloom, and beheld the most exquisite living being I had ever seen.

And as I watched my bride in wonder, delighting in her beauty and the open way she looked at me, eyes unafraid, my shadow broke free and surged for her, hungry, starving, ravenous.

It wrapped around her until she whimpered from terror.

CHAPTER 2

May

The room was dark. The blue fire burning in the middle didn't disperse the darkness, and I sat without moving, afraid I would stumble if I tried to walk somewhere. I wished the priestess turned on some brighter lights, but she was so brusque, so eager to leave me alone, I couldn't muster the energy to ask.

And she had no problem seeing in the gloom.

I didn't tell them about my night blindness. I omitted all of my issues, hoping against hope they would pick me before...

Before it was too late.

A miracle happened, and they did. And now I sat there, shaking from the cold in the darkness and wondering how angry my groom would be when he found out how frail, how weak I was.

Would he expect me to keep house for him? Or give him children at once? I hadn't bled in over a year, so I knew that was impossible at the moment, but if he gave me time... If he waited for me...

My breath shook when I reminded myself he had no reason to wait. In any way. And I shouldn't get my hopes up. After all, it was written in bold type in the fliers the temple gave me. *The marriage is invalid without consummation.*

He would want me right away. Tonight, probably. Unless he didn't want me at all. Maybe once he saw me, he would decide I was too ill, too ugly, too weak for him.

And maybe I'd be relieved by that.

I saw a troll earlier when I walked through the temple. Even now, the memory made my heart race painfully, and for a moment, the marrow-deep cold I always felt gave way to feverish nausea.

It couldn't be a troll, could it? He would crush me. My bones already broke easily, and to think that I would have to... That such a brutish, large creature would...

A creak of the door opening interrupted my growing panic, and I forced myself to gulp in a deep breath. My nervousness turned into a clammy fear, and I squinted, trying to make out the shape of whoever came in. No matter how hard I tried, I couldn't see *what* he was.

My breath hitched, my fear growing until my throat closed, my teeth chattering from terror.

I couldn't see in the gloom, but he could.

He'd see me now. He'd see me and decide I was hideous. Any moment now, he'd leave and tell the priestess he didn't want me, and I would spend the rest of my short life wondering what my perfect match looked like.

The door closed. Two bright blue lights turned on, focusing on me like flashlight beams. I gasped, closing my eyes instinctively. The cold, the fear, the fact I hadn't eaten since yesterday... All of it combined filled my head with buzzing, making my chest hurt, my body hollow.

I'd faint, I realized. And in case he still wanted me now, he would certainly leave after that. Who wanted a bride who couldn't stay conscious for her marriage ceremony?

And at that moment, when I tried to fight my body and keep myself from collapsing, knowing I'd fail, the strangest thing happened.

Something velvety smooth and warm wrapped around me like a blanket made of a light, delicate fabric. It wrapped around my palms, pressing into my freezing fingertips, going between my fingers to cushion the spaces between my hurting knuckles, and then racing up my arms, covering me with a delightful, thin layer of... something.

It wasn't a blanket or a fabric. As it covered more of my body, curving around my back, laying across my torso and stomach, enveloping my legs,

I realized the thing felt alive. It pulsed with something dark and hot, and for a moment, I was afraid.

But then...

I closed my eyes, breathing out a sigh of deep relief. Suddenly, I was warm. Not just warm. A hot, living energy soaked into my body, quenching the cold I always felt, soothing the tremors, making my heart's rhythm steadier.

I let out a small sound, a cry or a moan, and the blanket tightened around me. And I felt so very safe. As if wrapped in a cocoon of warm protection. It felt like I could finally sleep. Finally rest, knowing for sure I would wake up.

I hadn't had that luxury in so long.

"What's your name?" came a low, quiet voice.

It was a question, but the inflection was wrong. The voice was flat, the lilt at the end barely audible, and for a moment, I struggled to comprehend it.

My mind had grown so slow in recent months.

"May," I replied, no louder than a whisper.

"You're barely alive, May."

I cringed, a sob rising in my chest. He rejected me, just as I knew he would. But I didn't feel sad, not truly, when the delightful, warm presence ensconced me, its tendrils squeezing tight around me as if never to let go.

I didn't want them to. For the first time in years, I was truly warm, and it gave me strength.

Now that he was here and the dream of escaping the hell of my life became a reality, I was desperate for him to want me. And I knew I had little to entice him, but by gods, I would try. I would beg if I had to. Because there was no chance I was going back to... to that hell.

So I tried to plead my case. I had exactly one shot at securing this new life for myself, because once matched, I wouldn't be fit for anyone else. If he rejected me... I'd have to go back. And then, they would force me to bring in profit like the other girls did. I was an adult, after all. Adults had to work to earn their keep.

"Forgive me," I said. "I'll get better. I just need... a few weeks. It's not... It's not an illness. I'm not... I'm not contagious."

"That doesn't matter," came the voice, flat and without emotion.

Oh. My heart squeezed painfully. Of course, it didn't matter what my illness was. He didn't want a sick bride. I waited, knowing I'd hear him make his excuses any moment, knowing he'd go away, taking my last chance with him.

Seconds passed, punctuated by my shallow breaths. He was still here. Silent.

Why didn't he leave?

I refused to hope, but hope always found a way. It squeezed through the fissures in my frail self-control like grass squeezing through cracks in the pavement.

He's still here. Maybe he'll stay.

I opened my eyes and squinted, trying to penetrate the darkness. The flashlight beams were extinguished, and I couldn't see in the gloom, but it seemed to me the darkness grew thicker. The air was alive around me, fizzing with something, and it felt like a brewing storm.

He's like the storm, I thought, smiling with pleasure.

I loved rainy weather, and storms most of all. The crackle of lightning, the crash of thunder, and the untamed, violent electricity in the air. It was nature at its most primal, a force greater than any living thing. It filled me with awe.

I felt the same awe now, breathing in the charged air, basking in the presence of a force I could not see, but knew for certain was not human.

"Who are you?" I asked, breaking the heavy silence.

"I'm Virgil," he said.

Virgil. I bit my lip. That wasn't what I meant. I wanted to know his race, not his name, but I didn't quite know how to ask.

And yet, for now, the name was enough. It was

beautiful, and there was something sad in the way he said it.

"Nice to meet you, Virgil."

He feels like the storm and has a sad, melodic name, I thought, snuggling into the presence wrapped around me. It tightened more still, and I gave a low cry. It didn't hurt, but for the briefest moment, I felt as if it penetrated through my skin. Pushing deeper into my body. Inside me.

Two points of faint blue light lit just a few steps away, and I exhaled a nervous breath.

His eyes shine with light.

"You're beautiful, May," he said in that calm, expressionless voice.

I wasn't, but I wanted to return the compliment. Even more, I wanted to get up and walk toward him. Feel him with my fingers or try to find a light switch. I craved to see him.

"Thank you," I said after a moment and did not get up, my shyness holding me back. "You... You feel like the storm."

There was a rustle of fabric and a shuffle, and as the dark, humming presence around me tightened even more, pressing warmth and strength into my body, the shining eyes moved closer.

He was so close now. If I reached with my hand, I would touch him.

Instead, I inhaled, looking for his scent.

And it was strange. He smelled like... I concentrated, closing my eyes, and drew another breath.

Like fire, I realized. *Not like smoke, but like something burning. Pure and warm. And... and like the night air in autumn. Electrifying and ripe with memories of summer, preparing for the long sleep of winter.*

"Like the storm." He repeated my words, his voice sounding so close. "Why aren't you afraid, May? Are you so ill you can't feel fear?"

That took me by surprise. I blinked a few times, willing his shape to brighten against the gloom, but he remained obscured. I felt better now, the healthiest I felt in months, but it was deceptive. My eyes still didn't work. My body was still on the brink of giving out.

"Should I be afraid?" I asked, worried.

There was a dry sound, something akin to the bamboo chimes that hung around the small shrine by the orphanage, and the faint blue lights lowered. I guessed he crouched in front of me.

The warm darkness around me slithered over my skin, and I whimpered softly, the feeling surprisingly pleasant.

Indecently pleasant.

"No," he answered, his voice so close, I should have felt his breath on my face. I didn't. "I will never hurt you, May. Don't be afraid of me."

Right then, the door opened, and suddenly, light flooded the room. Someone turned on the switch.

I saw him right in front of me, so close, I startled.

My groom. My groom, who feels like the storm and smells like fire. My groom, who has eyes shining with light and no breath.

He's terrifying.

He was made of bone, his eyes two faint flames in his eye sockets. And yet, his head was not a skull.

He had a face.

I did nothing. I didn't scream, didn't move, didn't breathe.

And then, out of the corner of my eye, I saw the luxurious, shimmering darkness wrapped around me. It was like a translucent mantle, and I clearly saw now that it was an extension of him. It poured out of his chest, dark, shimmering tendrils of living shadow.

The shadowy tentacles gripped me, my entire body swallowed by his darkness.

"Get away from her!" came a panicked, high-pitched voice from the doorway.

CHAPTER 3

Virgil

I forced my shadow to let go of May. Little by little, it untangled from her and came back to me, quivering and hungry, as I slowly stood and faced the priestess. When I looked at her, she squeaked and covered her face with a black book she held.

"I acquainted myself with my bride," I said without reproach.

Truly, I suspected what it must have looked like. Those who knew anything about liches, knew about our shadows. About how we fed.

But the shadow had other functions. It was how we felt. How we connected. How we transferred energy.

Despite my rigid control, a tendril slipped out, hungry now that I fed all the heat and life I stored inside me into May. I batted it aside, determined not to scare the priestess. But I knew my instincts couldn't be kept at bay for long.

I needed to feed. Soon.

My eyes fell on the metal dish containing the eternal flame in the middle of the room. That fire was cold, but its energy was infinite. It tasted sharp and unpleasant, and since it gave off no heat, I couldn't use it to warm May's body.

No use feeding on it.

I would wait, then. Until we went outside and I could devour the torches.

May would need my support during the journey. I had to feed, not just to appease my shadow, but to keep her warm until we got to my home.

"Child, are you hurt?" the priestess called to May in a shaking voice, not daring to come closer. She hovered in the doorway, quaking with the slimy energy of fear.

"I'm fine," May said, her voice quiet yet clear.

After a moment, she looked up at me, her eyes wide, her lips parted. Her cheeks were unnaturally red, and her eyes shone, polished and glassy. Her features seemed so sharp and large against her delicate face with protruding cheekbones. Wispy hair framed her thin face, pale like her skin save for those red cheeks and lips.

She didn't look away, and I couldn't discern disgust on her face. She seemed surprised and curious, a bit childlike in the openness of her expression. But

I wasn't certain.

For the first time in ages, I wished I could read human expressions. I wanted to know what my bride thought. What she felt when she looked at me.

"Thank you," she said suddenly, not looking away from my face. "You made me feel warm."

I nodded and turned to the priestess, impatience urging me to hurry. May would be cold soon. We needed to complete the ceremony and leave so I could feed and keep her warm.

"Read the rites," I told the priestess, infusing my voice with power.

She flinched, terror flashing in her eyes, and came closer, as if pushed by an invisible force. The order I gave her was mild, just a compulsion, because she had to be sane of mind for the marriage to be valid.

But it was strong enough to move things along despite her fear.

"Come," I said, turning to May. "I will help you up."

I reached out my arm for her to take, and she hesitated, her lashes fluttering. I waited patiently, still amazed by her lack of fear. And as I waited, my shadow stirred, hungry for her. My body quivered with the hurting, hollow want, waiting for her touch to soothe it.

May took a deep breath, looked up, and gave me a sweet smile that loosened something in my chest.

"Thank you," she said, leaning on my arm.

Her touch was gentle and hesitant, her fingers trembling as she took hold of my forearm covered by the velvet sleeve. As she stood up, I realized how light she was. How weak.

How very precious.

I led her to the fire, going slowly to match her uncertain steps. We stood together opposite the priestess, and she watched us, her lips pursed to hide their trembling.

"May," she said, looking at my bride. "You can stop, you know. Some brides decide to leave when they see their grooms. You don't have a family to support, no need for his money, so you don't have to..."

"I do," May interrupted, her voice quiet. "I want to stay. Can we start, please?"

The hollow craving in my chest surged and swelled, and I hesitated, wanting to do something. To hold her.

I had seen this gesture plenty of times, but I never did it myself.

Slowly, I took May's hand off my forearm. When she looked up with curious eyes, I put my arm around her back, nervousness churning inside me. I was afraid she would startle or bolt, and so I tightened my hold little by little, offering her support and letting the feel of her soothe the abyss inside me.

May's breath stuttered, and she looked down, blushing, but she didn't run. Instead, she leaned on me, taking the support I offered.

I let my shadow out through my forearm so the priestess wouldn't see it, and pressed it into the small of May's back. She gasped softly, lips parting.

"Very well. I have a translation of lich wedding rites here," the priestess said without stuttering now that the power of compulsion urged her on. "Obviously, I can't do it in the original language. May wouldn't understand a word, and me, neither."

"Please, continue," I said, eager for this to be done.

Touching May with my body and shadow filled me with pleasure, and it was strange and intimate, something I wanted to explore in private.

The priestess cleared her throat and opened the book, smoothing down the page with trembling fingers.

"Here are two souls who wish to tie their fates in an eternal union," she said, and I let my eyes dim, taking pleasure in the words.

Even translated, they were still beautiful.

"Two stars that will shine brightly over the penumbra of time. Two lovers who vow to become one."

May exhaled softly, her body shifting against me, and I tightened my hold. Even though I knew nothing about her, only her name and how fragile she was, I would make my vow with confidence.

She would have my soul forever, until we lay down together for eternal sleep.

"May, look at your groom and repeat after me."

I let her go, and she turned to me, looking up shyly. Even though the rite didn't call for holding hands, she gripped my palm in hers, a small frown appearing on her face.

I knew why she was confused. To feel the smooth, warm bone of my hand under her fingers must be startling.

May looked down at our hands, gently brushing her thumb over my knuckles, and an electric wave of pleasure surged through me until I swayed on my feet.

She touched my body without fear or disgust. She didn't run.

My bride looked up, a gentle smile on her face, and murmured, "You are what I was required to be but couldn't. It feels like fate, somehow."

Before I could understand what she meant, the priestess read her vow, and May repeated, looking up into my eyes.

"I vow to accompany you in your eternal journey," she said, her voice quiet but clear. Unhesitant. "I will stay by your side in light and in dark, welcome you in my soul and my body, eat from your shadow, and bear the fruit of our union. As I stand here, I offer myself to you, Virgil. All my futures are in your hands."

"I vow to accompany you in your eternal journey," I said my vow, looking into her gray eyes beholding me with sweet openness. "I will stay by your side in light and in dark, welcome you in my soul and my body, feed you from my shadow and hand. I will lie with you, wake with you, stay with you. You have my protection and my eternal promise, May. All my futures are in your hands."

And then, because the vow didn't sit quite right in my mouth, I repeated it in my native tongue. The ancient language, almost forgotten now that liches were so few, resounded in the wedding chamber, filling it with mellifluous cadence, the words joining into one, unbroken song. Quiet and strong, it wrapped around us all, my shadow making the sound reverberate and spread over the chamber, the song of my vow swelling with emotion.

When I finished, May had tears in her eyes, and I wondered if she was sad.

"It was beautiful," she whispered, putting me at ease. "Thank you."

Even the priestess seemed awed when she finally said, "You are joined for eternity. Congratulations."

CHAPTER 4

May

"**M**ay, if you need anything..." the priestess began when we were about to go.
But Virgil didn't let her finish. His hard arm was wrapped around my back, skeletal fingers pressing into my waist. His voice sounded harsh when he answered the priestess.

"I will take care of my wife's every need."

She faltered and looked away with a sigh. Finally, she looked up, gave me a false smile, and congratulated us once again.

"If you'll excuse me. I have another couple scheduled."

She left quickly, looking very much like she was running away. I glanced at Virgil's face, just for a moment, because now that we were married, I felt awfully shy.

I found him already looking at me.

"Are you strong enough to travel?" he asked, his face cold and expressionless. It was like a sculpture made from the purest marble, and yet, I suspected it was bone. Even his lips seemed hard, and yet, they moved when he spoke. Was it magic?

I still didn't know what race he belonged to, only that I'd never seen anyone like him.

"Um, I think so," I said. "But… I haven't eaten."

I said it shamefully. I knew I had to eat now that I left the orphanage. That I chose not to, even though the temple offered me breakfast this morning, was something that confused me. Yet, a part of me suspected why I'd done it.

Ugly. Fat. Misshapen. You're but a slimy, disgusting larva, May. When will the butterfly emerge?

Those words echoed in my head very loud the morning of my wedding. So I didn't eat. It pacified the voices.

But now that I asked for food, they grew loud again, and my breathing turned shallow as I tried to silence them. Virgil stood by my side, his arm supporting me still, and I leaned on him, trying to draw strength from his touch.

You're beautiful, May.

I hoped he really thought so, even if I knew he was wrong. Maybe he wouldn't mind it if I ate just a little.

"I'll feed you," Virgil said, his voice cool, face expressionless. "Come now. Can you walk?"

I nodded, and to my relief, he didn't withdraw his arm. We walked slowly out of the wedding chamber, my groom supporting my every step. He stopped just outside the doors and looked around.

"No one's here. Please, don't be frightened."

I didn't know what to make out of this until suddenly, a cloud of glittering darkness burst out of him. It raced down the corridor, long tentacles unfurling and reaching for the torches on both walls. I watched, mesmerized.

As a glittery tendril of shadow wrapped around the nearest torch, its fire grew brighter, then dimmed and brightened again. The flames rose and fell, seeming to struggle, and finally gave a sharp sizzle, as if a cry.

I startled. For a moment, it seemed like the flame was fighting... Until it went out, completely extinguished, not even a wisp of smoke left in its place.

The same thing happened to each torch down the wall, flames going out one by one, until we were plunged into darkness.

I swayed on my feet, unsettled by what I saw. Only Virgil's arm kept me steady.

"There. You'll be warm now," he murmured.

The soft, consuming blanket that warmed me up

earlier wrapped around me, a pulsing heat and powerful energy rushing into my body until I cried out, trying to tear myself out of its grip. It was as if a hot, living fire was forced into my body, setting me ablaze. I was burning alive, but there was no light, no smoke, nothing in the darkness that hid us after Virgil strangled the torches.

My skin and insides burned and a fever seized my limbs. I felt sick, dizzy, like my body was too tight for me, my bones hot embers destroying me from within.

It stopped instantly, and Virgil held me closer, his chest steady under my cheek.

"Too fast," he said, his voice heated with something I couldn't name. "Forgive me. I got... excited."

I shivered, confused and frightened, but he was steady and unmoving against me. The pain was gone, but I still shook, my breathing fast and shallow.

And if he was excited, why didn't his breath wheeze just as fast as mine? Why didn't his chest move under my cheek?

Why was his heart quiet?

That was when I understood it fully. My groom did not breathe. He didn't have a beating heart in his chest.

He wasn't alive, and yet he walked, talked, and held

me.

I slowly calmed down, my body buzzing with energy, pleasant warmth radiating from my belly out. I wasn't hot or cold any longer, just pleasantly warm in a way I didn't recall ever feeling. And Virgil was warm, too, despite not being alive, so I burrowed into his embrace.

Whatever he was... I couldn't think about it. I was too weak, my mind too slow, so I pushed it all away and took the comfort he offered.

Held tight in Virgil's arms, I soaked in the warmth.

"I'm sorry," he said, his hard face gently pressing into the top of my head. "I took in too much. I was so eager... Doesn't matter. I'll be more careful in the future. Did it hurt very much?"

I still didn't understand what he meant and what just happened, but I shook my head and gripped the fabric of his luxurious, velvet jacket in my hands.

He was warm. He was strong. Even more, he was the only person who wanted me and touched me willingly. Tears gathered in my eyes, all the anxiety and terror I felt before the wedding wanting out.

Virgil was careful with me. He cared about me. It was so much better than I dared to hope for.

"I'm not in pain," I said, fighting to keep my tears from spilling onto his beautiful jacket. "But, um... I can't see in the dark. I'm sorry. There are a few things wrong with me, and I didn't tell..."

"May," he interrupted, pressing me closer. "You are ill, but there's nothing wrong with you. And it's all right. I can see for us both. Do I have your permission to carry you? Just until we're out of the dark."

His voice wasn't as comforting as his touch. Still cold and flat, seemingly with no emotion, it made it difficult for me to understand his words. It was as if with the inflection lacking, his words lost meaning.

I really had to eat soon, if only to heal my mind.

"Yes, you can carry me," I said, my heart thumping hard.

Virgil let go of me and leaned closer, and then put his arm under my knees, the other on my back. He hoisted me up without a groan, a breath, or any indication of effort.

I whimpered in pain, the hard bone of his arm digging into the backs of my thighs, and he adjusted his hold, making it better.

"Just until we're in the light," he whispered.

I put my hands around his neck, hesitantly, because I hadn't been carried before, and we set out. Virgil was so quiet. Now that I was in the arms of someone who didn't breathe, I realized how many sounds a living body really made.

His did not, and it was eerie. I wondered if Virgil

was alive.

Did it matter? He was warm, and strong, and despite the pain of bone pressing into bone, I felt so good in his arms. Safe and cared for. For the briefest moment, all the voices in my head were silent, and I was just a girl carried by her groom.

So normal and sweet, I could cry.

"There you go," Virgil said, slowly letting me go until my feet were planted on the ground. "We'll pass through the portal now."

He took the lead, rushing us through the bustling temple, holding my hand firmly. I only had time enough to look around one last time, terrified and startled faces flashing around me as Virgil pulled me behind him, so much faster now that we were among people.

I heard gasps and something that sounded like a sob. When I turned, I saw a woman watching me with wide eyes, a handkerchief pressed to her lips.

Before I could make sense of that, we were by the portals, and Virgil recited coordinates to a pale, stuttering man who operated the passage.

I wondered if the man was always so nervous. Or only when Virgil spoke to him.

When we emerged from the portal on the other side, it was on a quiet road that seemed to be on the outskirts of a town. Numerous chimneys smoked in the distance, but where we were, only a few buildings stood away from the road.

There was no one around, just a beautiful black carriage waiting by the portal. I looked at it in awe, because I had only seen such things in books. It seemed fit for a prince... Until I noticed that the carriage was not drawn by horses.

Instead, two skeletal horse-sized creatures waited, motionless, their eye sockets burning with a purple fire.

"Get in, May," Virgil said, motioning at the carriage door that opened on its own, as if by magic. "Let's go home."

CHAPTER 5

Virgil

May sat opposite me, her face turned to the window. I wondered if she wanted to look at the landscape or avoid seeing my face. Maybe it was both.

In the temple, I tried to move fast so she wouldn't see other people's reactions to me. I failed. There were sounds of distress and terrified looks, and she saw all of that.

Before May, I had never paid much attention to how living beings reacted to me. Now, I was worried. What if she took her cue from them and feared me as well? Humans did everything collectively, I noticed. If one was afraid, the entire crowd would soon be, too.

"How do you feel?" I asked, trying my hardest to make my voice soothing.

When she flinched and turned to me with an upset expression, I cursed myself. Of course, she was afraid now.

"I just… I know you made me warm, and I appreciate it," she said, looking directly at my face. "Thank you. It's just that… I should eat."

She looked away, her cheeks reddened, and I cursed myself again. Here I was, worrying selfishly about how she saw me, while my bride was simply hungry. All those lessons I'd taken seemed to have done me no good. In the excitement of having her by my side, I forgot that humans needed other kinds of sustenance, not just pure energy.

I never had a human being under my direct care. Not until now. But that was no excuse to forget my bride's physical needs.

The way I fed her through my shadow would keep her warm and young. It wouldn't feed her body the way it needed to stay strong and healthy.

At least, the fire's energy wouldn't.

"We can stop in town," I said, even though it meant she would see more reactions, more reasons to fear me. "I will buy you food. What would you like?"

"Bread," she said at once. "Milk. And…"

But she lowered her eyes again, shaking her head, her face really red. She curled in on herself, and I wondered if what she felt was shame or fear.

"What is it?" I asked, tired of guessing.

"Nothing," May said, shaking her head again.

"Bread and milk. Thank you."

The carriage rocked, jostling us, and I leaned forward, gently reaching for her. I took her chin between my finger and thumb and slowly turned her face to me.

"Are you afraid of me, May?" I asked, willing her expression to make sense to me.

"No!" she said, so forcefully, I let go of her at once. "That's not... Well, I am a bit wary, but that's not what I..."

She broke off, letting out a sharp breath, and shook her head again.

"It's just that I really want to have some honey," she said, looking stubbornly at her hands wringing in her lap. "Just a little bit, to dip the bread in. And I shouldn't. I'm really sorry. I won't bring it up again."

I didn't answer, watching her with confusion. We were getting close to the market square, and I would soon have to go out and buy the food she wanted. And if she liked honey, I wanted to get it for her.

"Does honey make you sick? Is that why you shouldn't have it?" I asked, looking at my nervous, blushing bride with utmost focus.

She shook her head, giving me a startled look.

"No! It's just... Girls like me shouldn't have sweet things. That's all."

"Girls like you...?"

She released a long breath and clenched her hands into fists, refusing to look at me. The carriage stopped, having reached the market square. I looked outside, trying to gauge how busy it was.

Not too many people around. Good.

"So you like honey and it doesn't make you sick," I said, trying to make sense of our conversation.

May buried her face in her hands and made a sound of discomfort. "Yes," came her muffled voice. "But..."

"Please, stay inside," I said and left the carriage.

I headed for the bakery first, beckoning my invisible servants who drove the carriage to follow me. I bought a dozen currant buns for May, and then added a loaf of bread to my order, remembering she requested it.

Maybe she didn't like buns. But I wanted to get her the best, and when I asked the baker which of his wares people liked the most, he told me, stuttering, that the currant buns were the most popular.

I got her cookies decorated with sugar, as well. Another ware the baker swore was a favorite among the town humans.

His hands barely shook when he packed everything into bags, and I tipped him for his helpfulness, asking where I could get the freshest milk and the sweetest honey.

When I returned to the carriage a quarter of an hour later, my servants in tow, lugging heavy bags, I stopped suddenly, worried.

May stood next to the carriage, speaking to two village women. Her back was to me, but their faces were clearly visible, both expressive with strong emotions.

So this is it, I thought, morose and a bit angry. *They told her what I am. She will request that I let her go now.*

Or maybe she would simply run from me. When humans were terrified, they ran.

For the briefest moment, I wondered if May was strong enough to run. If she weren't... maybe I would have another chance. I would take her with me to help her regain her health, and in the meantime, maybe I could show her she had nothing to fear from me.

It was selfish, I knew, but she was my bride. I hoped one could be a bit selfish about one's bride.

One of the women spotted me and her face twisted into the familiar expression.

Fear. Disgust.

Both women turned away, retreating hastily, and May looked after them, her slight body straight, her shoulders square. I couldn't see her face, and it worried me even more.

"I asked you to stay inside," I said, letting her know from a distance I was coming so she wouldn't be startled.

May still flinched, and then turned, looking at me with those wide, innocent eyes.

"I'm sorry," she said, giving no indication of planning to run. I relaxed. "They came up to the carriage when they saw you were gone. They were curious, I think, and got scared when they saw me. I think they expected the carriage to be empty. So I came out to talk to them."

I nodded, motioning for my servants to load the bags inside. May startled when she saw the bags moving seemingly on their own.

"My servants are invisible," I told her at once, trying to alleviate her fear. "They are harmless. And they'll obey you, too, you just need to say what you need. I bought... well, many things. Maybe you could do your shopping next time. When you're stronger. I'll accompany you."

Again, my selfishness. I didn't want to go with her only to help her. I needed to keep an eye on the townspeople so they wouldn't try to scare my lovely bride away.

May nodded, and I came over to help her back in the carriage. I offered her my hand to lean on, and she took it, her unafraid touch stirring the fire I consumed earlier into a bit of a frenzy.

If liches could blush, I would. May certainly blushed for us both.

As I followed her inside, I noticed a small crowd gathering around the two women who talked to May. They were pointing fingers at us and waving their hands, and my soul darkened with anger.

I really hoped they wouldn't make May feel unwelcome the next time we came here. If they did... I might just indulge my anger.

For now, though, I put them out of my mind and sat with my bride.

"My home is an hour away from town," I said. "Would you like to eat something now?"

When she nodded, I gave her a bun, and we set out.

By the time we arrived, May still hadn't finished her food, nibbling daintily on the smallest crumbs she could tear off. I watched her with confusion, wondering if that was how people ate. When I was hungry, I devoured whatever I could reach with my shadow, and soon, I'd do just that. The insubstantial energy from the fire was almost spent. I needed something that would keep.

But maybe May was different.

"Here we are," I said when the carriage stopped in front of the manor's main entrance. "I'll show you inside and then, I'll have to take a walk. I apologize for leaving you alone. I'll be back shortly."

She nodded, and I led her up the stairs to the front

door, holding her trembling hand in mine.

Watch over her, I instructed my servants. *Don't let her run away from me.*

CHAPTER 6

May

He lived in a palace. That was the only word that could give his home justice.

As Virgil led me inside, holding my hand in his bony, warm one, I walked slowly, trying to absorb the magnitude of the place.

The building was big and tall, with at least three high-ceilinged floors under the gently sloping roof. Its façade was of gray stone, and parts of it were covered in ivy and ramblers, some of them reaching as high as the roof.

I only saw the front before we entered, and it glittered with a multitude of clean, glassed windows. The late September sun reflected in them as if in jewels, and that alone was a sign of extravagant opulence.

In the orphanage, we had to make do with oiled paper stretched taut between the window frames.

In winter, we covered the windows with cardboard and wood planks if we could get any.

The steps leading up to the double front door were of black marble veined with white, and Virgil's hold on my hand tightened when we climbed them.

"They are slippery when wet," he murmured, glancing at me. "I'll have them covered in the future."

"No!" I burst out, so awed, I spoke without thinking. "They are so beautiful. It would be a shame to cover them on my account."

He stopped in front of the door, in the shadow of an awning, and turned to me, cradling my hands in his. I blushed when his burning eyes focused on my face, two blue, vivid flames shining in the shade.

"Then you'll have to promise never to leave without my assistance," he said quietly.

A shiver ran down my spine, and for a moment, I was afraid. There was such a strange intensity in his eyes and posture. He bowed slightly over me, and though his body was lean and impeccably clothed, it radiated power and something primal and threatening I couldn't name.

We were so close. My hands were trapped in his.

Breath stuttering in sync with my palpitating heart, I braved his gaze and swallowed, forcing my tight throat to loosen.

"I promise," I said, and Virgil nodded, his face impassive.

I couldn't tell what he felt, and that unsettled me even more than his predatory aura. But then he led me inside, the doors flying open when we turned toward them, and I got distracted, the house consuming my attention.

The floor in the entrance hall was a smooth, polished mosaic of tiny black and white tiles. A grand staircase led up to the second floor, ending in a gallery that overlooked the enormous entrance hall. And up, over my head, a glittering chandelier tinkled gently, the crystals moved by the breeze we let in through the open door.

I sighed with awe, slowly looking left and right. There was art on the walls, beautiful landscapes depicting flowers, trees, animals, and the sky, overcast in every painting, with silver light shining through the clouds.

Sculptures were tastefully arranged around the hall, making the cavernous space seem less empty without crowding it.

All were made of white marble and depicted mostly animals. A deer running, its hooves seeming to fly over its plinth. A tiger caught mid-leap. Another animal, something similar to a rabbit, but much larger, cowering in fear. And a human woman covering her face with a raised arm, as if blinded.

I wanted to take a closer look at her, because there was something unsettling in her posture, but Virgil gently pulled my hand, and I followed him.

"Some facilities were added when I requested a bride through the temple," he said, leading me left. "There is a kitchen, and it's new. As for bathrooms, we added... the amenities humans need. You should be comfortable."

The black and white tiles gave way to polished wood that gleamed in the light falling in through the windows. Everything in this house seemed somehow bare, no carpets covering the floors, no curtains or drapes over the windows. It had a strange austerity to it despite the art displayed in each room.

And everything was unnaturally clean, as if brand new.

"The kitchen," Virgil said, showing me into a spacious room on the far left side of the mansion. "You can now eat in more dignified conditions than the carriage. There is a bathroom down the corridor if you need to freshen up. And I'll be back soon."

"Thank you," I said, looking around with wide eyes.

The kitchen was much simpler and seemed more modern than the rest of the house, which had an aura of timelessness about it. There was a fridge humming quietly in the corner, an oven, a sink with a gleaming tap, and so many cabinets. I couldn't imagine I'd ever have enough food to fill them up.

I couldn't even guess how much it must have cost to create this scape. Electricity was so expensive, only the wealthiest could afford it, and so appliances like the refrigerator were rare. I knew what it was from books.

In the orphanage, we made do with candles and human labor.

A sturdy wooden table stood by the window, a plate already prepared. A tall glass of milk waited by the plate, and I swallowed.

I'll eat, I swore to myself. *It's all right now.*

Virgil was already out the door when he stopped and slowly walked back.

"You'll be here when I return. Will you?" he asked, and for a moment, I thought he was uncertain.

"Of course," I answered. "Where else would I go?"

He nodded, not looking at me, and clasped his hands in front of him, thinking. Finally, he looked up, and I gasped softly. His eyes were no longer blue, but a light, warm orange.

"May I kiss you before I go?"

I didn't answer him at once. My mouth went

dry, and my heart thumped so hard, I was afraid it would bruise me on the inside. I just stood there, frozen, looking at the creature who was my husband. Who had rights to me now.

To my kisses, to my body, to my everything.

Before, I didn't fully comprehend what it meant to be married. He was so kind, and touched me in ways that were friendly or caring, and now...

My heart hammered, and my insides twisted when the voices surged in my head like a crescendo.

Ugly. No one will ever want you. Who would touch this fat body? Who would look twice at your disgusting plump face?

I was silent for too long, my body's violent response and the buzzing in my head distracting me.

"You can say no," Virgil said quietly, the glow of his eyes dimming until it was almost extinguished. "I'm sorry. I didn't mean to..."

"No!" I interrupted, taking a step forward.

Shut up! I told the voices, and since I did that so rarely, they obeyed.

I was out now. Out of the orphanage. And that meant, I had to purge it out of myself, as well.

This was my husband. My new life. My future. I would kiss him and give him whatever he desired, because I never wanted him to stop needing things from me.

Needing me.

"I'm sorry, I... Yes, Virgil. Please, kiss me."

His eyes lit up, even brighter than before, and he came closer in slow, measured steps. I trembled, looking up at his bony face that had no expression save for his burning eyes. But the way he moved showed purpose, and for the first time since I saw him, I felt hope.

Maybe I would learn to read him with time. Maybe he had tells just like everyone, only different from the human ones. If so, I would learn to decipher them.

Virgil stood so close, the tips of his shoes touched mine. I looked up, suddenly breathless and hot with a stifling, expectant emotion.

He lifted his hands gently and cupped my face. I was prepared so I didn't flinch when the smooth, warm bone pressed against my skin, though my pulse picked up, rushing faster and faster.

"I've never kissed anybody," he whispered, and his eyes dimmed again, the orange turning into a deep, smoke-tinged red.

It would have been horrifying if I wasn't so captivated by his confession.

"I haven't, either," I whispered back.

"We'll learn together, then," he said, lowering his

face to mine. "Close your eyes."

I did, and as soon as my mind plunged into the darkness behind my eyelids, my other senses sharpened. His fingers brushed my skin gently, making me shiver. His touch wasn't unpleasant, but it made me feel feverish, my body vibrating with anticipation.

He has lips, passed through my mind. *But they seem to be made of bone. How does it work? How will it feel?*

Virgil moved closer, which I sensed from the quality of the air pressing against my mouth. He didn't breathe, so there was no other movement from him. Just the air he stirred with his body.

I breathed fast, so fast I was dizzy, and when something smooth and hard pressed into my lower lip, my body jolted, my breath rushing out of me.

It wasn't yet the kiss. He simply touched his finger to my lip, and it made me tingle from head to toe.

"They are so red," he whispered right in front of me, so close, I would have felt his breath if he was alive. "So soft. I feel your blood thrumming, May. Your heart beats so fast. Are you afraid?"

My breath hitched in my throat, making a sound like a squeak, and he brushed his finger lower, caressing my chin.

"I-It's not fear, I think," I said, my voice so quiet, I almost didn't hear it over the rushing of blood in my ears. "I think I'm just nervous."

"Nervous," he repeated, pressing his finger right in the middle of my lower lip, so firmly, he rolled it down, baring my lower teeth. "Is it a good or a bad feeling?"

I swallowed thickly, and he let go of my lip.

"It's both," I said truthfully. "But... I'm usually nervous when I'm waiting for something important."

The air shifted again, his hands settled on my cheeks, and suddenly, hard bone brushed against my parted lips.

"Important," he repeated, his mouth moving against mine. "Yes, it is."

He kissed me.

And with his kiss, a terrible, suffocating darkness poured into me like the storm.

CHAPTER 7

Virgil

A s my mouth pressed to hers, my shadow shot out, eager to wrap around her. For a moment, I hesitated. I was hungry. What if I instinctively fed off her? May didn't have much to give. She'd be dead, sucked dry before I could stop myself.

The thought she would be no more filled me with sadness, but the idea of drinking her shimmering, moth-like energy, of taking her into myself...

It stirred my hunger and made my shadow leap for her and tighten around May's body in a strangling hold. She whimpered against my mouth, and I squeezed tighter still, temptation and desire taking over.

As I hovered there, on the edge between two pleasures, possessing May with my mouth or with my being, her lips moved against mine.

She kissed me with hesitant gentleness, and I

made a sound, something primal and soft in the depths of my chest. My shadow released her, caressing now instead of gripping, soothing her nervous flesh, pouring into her instead of taking.

She tasted like a meadow of wildflowers on a summer evening. Like startled fireflies taking to the sky at midnight. Like rain and fire, and the sweet spirits of butterflies and bees.

May tasted like life itself.

My hunger shifted, the need to consume becoming a craving to possess. I devoured her with my mouth as my shadow moved over her limbs and pressed against her skin, wrapping her whole in a web of my being.

She made a choked sound that seemed to express suffering, and yet, her mouth tasted mine and her arms were around my neck, fingers pressing into my hair, fluttery and hesitant.

As my shadow enveloped her, my arms went around her, pressing her to me, fingers smoothing up and down her back. I felt the bone of her spine, the shifting weight of her muscles, and then deeper, the blood rushing in her veins.

I broke the kiss and held her closer, laying my cheek on her head, and she trembled in my arms, her breath like that of a terrified animal fleeing from a predator.

That was what we were, and I was so acutely aware

of this truth, it hurt my very soul.

She was the prey. I was the predator. And her body knew to fear me, even if May herself was so warped, so broken, she didn't understand it.

Or maybe I was wrong. Maybe the hearts of living things could beat in lust as strongly as they did in terror. Maybe her body was broken, too, her survival instinct malfunctioning.

"Still nervous?" I asked, trying to smooth my energies, tearing my shadow away from her with force that made me hurt.

"No," May breathed against my chest. "I'm... feverish. I think. Hot. But... It feels good."

Were her instincts damaged or could she see past my nature and want me despite it? I didn't know. And I was selfish enough not to care.

When she gave herself to me, I didn't want to be noble and question whether it was a sane decision. Of course, it wasn't. No animal in its right mind would come to me of its own volition. I knew this and still decided not to care, not to set May straight and explain it was more reasonable to fear me than embrace me.

Whatever she gave, I would take. Hopefully, I would stop before taking too much.

"Thank you," I said, letting her go with regret. "Please, eat something. I should be back in an hour."

I left her with more ease now. No longer worried she might bolt when given the chance, I set my servants to watch over her and went to hunt.

When I returned, brimming with sweet, living energy that would last me weeks, she was still in the kitchen. My servants reported she had spent some time in the bathroom, and then drank her milk and ate bread with honey in slow bites.

When I entered, I saw her sitting in her chair and looking at her plate, on which a single sugar cookie sat. She seemed determined, her posture straight, her eyes intense.

"I'm back," I said softly.

She pushed away from the table and stood in front of me, blushing. She didn't look at me, just at the floor, and I wondered why.

"What is the emotion you feel now?" I asked her, curious.

The good thing was, once she told me, I would remember and know the next time when she behaved the same way.

May startled, glancing at the table, and then at me. She pressed her lips together, her blush deepening.

"I... It's called shame, I think."

"Why are you ashamed?" I asked, my curiosity growing. "Has something happened?"

I should have stayed by her side, I chided myself. *I*

missed something important.

"I am ashamed because I want this cookie, but I'm afraid if I have one, I will want more."

She said that fast, still not looking at me, and my confusion grew. There it was. May having strong emotions about human food. Just as she did with the honey.

"What's wrong with having more than one cookie?" I asked, coming a step closer to block her way out of the room in case she found my questions too uncomfortable.

May glanced at me, wringing her hands together, and shook her head slightly.

"The explanation is ugly and wrong, and I shouldn't even think it. This is my new life. I should let go of the old. I'm sorry."

"Don't apologize when you did nothing wrong," I said, coming closer until I could touch her.

She was fascinating, and the fact she tried to hide something from me, raising walls of shame and furtive glances between us, made my curiosity burn bright. Now fed and content, I had all the time in the world to lavish May with attention.

I would uncover all her secrets.

"Tell me the ugly explanation," I said, putting my hands on her shoulders.

May's face shifted, mouth twisting this way and

that, and I memorized every twitch of her features. These were the signs of secrets she kept from me. I needed to know them so I could get the truth out of her whenever she behaved this way.

"Because cookies will make me fat," she said quickly, as if forcing the words out. "And I'm ugly as it is."

I was confused and irritated. It was clearly not the case.

"Don't lie to me," I said, and she flinched, looking up with wide eyes. "You are beautiful. Don't ever call yourself ugly again."

She startled, her lips parting, and just looked at me with that open expression. Her eyes were wide, mouth open, nostrils flaring. As if she took me in with all her senses, much more intensely than normal.

"As for the cookies, the baker assured me his wife eats them in excess. And I don't know about fat or not, because I don't pay much attention to that, but her life energy is healthy, robust and bright, and this is what I want for you. Do you think the cookies will make you weaker than you are now? Is this why you're worried?"

It was a genuine question, but May suddenly smiled, shaking her head.

"No," she said, her eyes crinkling at the corners. "I think they might make me better."

"Have the cookie, then. If you dislike it, I won't be offended. If you like it and eat all of them, we'll go to town to get more."

I let go of her shoulders, and May nodded, her eyes cast down. Her lovely face was rosy with a blush, and as she turned away, facing the table with her back to me, even the tips of her ears tinted red.

She reached for the cookie, and then I heard quiet crunching noises. She ate slowly, not letting me see, and tried to be quiet. I wondered why that was, but then, I realized I did the same thing.

Did I not keep myself from hunting on the way back here for fear of what she'd think if she saw it? Did I not go only when I knew she wouldn't follow? Maybe she was like me, afraid her feeding habits would disgust me.

Not that they would. Nothing May did would revolt me. But I could give her this privacy since I allowed it to myself, as well.

She finished the cookie, had a sip of milk, and gathered her plate and glass. I put my hand on her shoulder, and she startled slightly.

"Leave it. The servants will clean. Now come with me. I have many things to show you."

CHAPTER 8

May

I was drowsy after eating, and yet, I had so much more energy than usual. It helped me reason away the voices and put up with the feeling of my stomach being full. A forbidden, naughty feeling that made my skin crawl with shame...

I pushed that thought away.

It wasn't like I never used to eat in the orphanage. We had three meals a day, but our portions were rigidly controlled. Madame Sundara weighed the food herself, checking a chart she made every week to give each girl the proper amount of food.

Those who were scheduled to perform received less. And I performed often. Unlike most girls, I enjoyed dancing, and Madame, in an unusual moment of kindness, told me once I had a natural talent.

So that was why I was so unused to the feeling

of fullness. Why my hands sweated now and my body felt bloated and sick.

But I wasn't going to perform anymore, was I? That was behind me. It was fine to eat, then. I would get used to feeling sated.

Virgil had my arm in the crook of his elbow, his steps slow and adjusted to my pace as we climbed the stairs. On the first floor, he led me to a set of rooms on the right side of the house—the west wing. My heart beat fast, not from exertion, but from anxiety.

I suspected he was leading me to the bedroom.

When a set of white doors with gilded frames opened at our approach, I stopped, my feet refusing to go on.

I saw the enormous bed inside. It was covered with dark sheets, partly hidden from view by a sheer fabric hanging from the canopy, pinned up to one side.

Virgil turned to face me.

"This is your room, May."

His voice was unusually gentle. I looked up, trying to glean understanding from his face, but it was impassive as always.

"Um... Thank you," I said, fidgeting. "And are you... going in?"

"Yes."

I stepped from foot to foot, a wave of nervousness pouring over me. So this was it. The wedding night, as expected.

I glanced at the window at the end of the corridor, and indeed, the sky was colored with dusky pinks and purples, the sun already set.

All right, then. I could do it. After all, I knew from the start what a marriage would entail. I knew I'd marry a stranger and have to lie with him.

But now that I knew who my husband was, how scared people were of him, and that they called him a lich with terror and an odd reverence, like those two women in town did... It suddenly seemed so much worse.

The only consolation was that he wasn't a troll. Virgil was of a masculine yet lean build, and there was grace and carefulness to his movements. He wouldn't crush me.

And then there was... the kiss.

If this were anything like that kiss, I thought, relaxing slightly, *then maybe it wouldn't be that bad. Maybe I wouldn't suffer like the girls in the orphanage said.*

It hurts so much, May. Like someone's tearing you apart.

I pushed the voice away, shivering, and made myself focus on less frightening things.

So... the kiss.

The feel of those hard yet warm lips on my face. Virgil's mouth was dry, and yet, it seemed to warm and soften the longer it touched mine. And his taste was so pleasant and so... magical. He tasted like fire, a fragrant flame, like warmth and security, and something else. Something dark and hungry, which excited my blood and made it rush to my head and hips.

The memory made my heart flutter, butterflies taking flight in my stomach, and I looked up at Virgil.

Maybe I wouldn't mind it at all if he lay with me. If his strong hands came around my body in the rustling darkness of the bedroom. If he pressed me close, kissing me some more, and showed me the body underneath his clothes...

"What are you thinking, May?" he asked, tilting his head to the side.

I hiccupped, startled and embarrassed. I was quiet for too long, kept him waiting in the doorway, and just now, I looked at him while thinking about seeing him naked.

So indecent.

I looked away, my face heating, and worried my lower lip. He forbade me from lying, and that was a relief. He shouldn't be angry if I told him the truth.

"I thought about... whether now is the time for... our wedding night."

My hands wouldn't be still. I couldn't look at him, because my embarrassment was like a hot fire, so I didn't know how he reacted. Then again, his face usually didn't convey anything. Apart from the glow in his eyes changing color.

I glanced up, just to check, and sure enough—his eyes were orange.

"Not yet, May," he said, voice expressionless. "I'd like you to feel comfortable first."

A surprised gasp burst out of me. He said no when I already braced myself, already prepared and even looked forward to it. Now, I was oddly disappointed. Relieved, too, but even more... dissatisfied.

Most of all, I was just surprised he thought I would grow comfortable with time. To me, it seemed impossible. But if he believed that, maybe there was hope.

I looked up, and Virgil's eyes slowly returned to their blue color as he watched me without speaking.

"That's very kind," I said to fill the silence.

"Is it? I simply thought it prudent. I will want to come to your bed often, May. It wouldn't be healthy for you to be uncomfortable every time."

"Oh."

I looked away, blushing. So he wanted me. And he held himself back... so I wouldn't be afraid.

"I still believe it's kind," I said softly, giving him a shy smile.

Virgil's eyes flashed a bit brighter, and then his mouth curved up slowly, the corners lifting. The rest of his face did not shift, just his mouth, so it took me a moment to realize he tried to smile.

It looked eerie and wrong, and yet... I wondered if he did that to imitate my expression. To make me feel more at ease.

"The lights will be lit soon," he said after a moment, the smile still fixed on his face. "And I wanted to show you your wardrobe. It was prepared ahead of time, and my servants will gradually adjust it to fit you better. For now, I just hoped you would choose a dress to wear tomorrow. They can tailor it for you through the night."

"Oh. Thank you," I said, blushing again.

He was so thoughtful. A warm, pleasant sensation rose in my stomach, and I touched Virgil's arm, brushing my fingers over the fabric of his clothes. It was velvet, I knew. Soft, plushy, and so much nicer than the thin, threadbare fabrics I was used to.

The dress I wore was a drab, gray thing that frayed at the hem. I couldn't wait to wear something else. Something that would do a better job keeping me warm, for example.

"So come in. I know it's selfish of me, but I wanted to study your reactions. I was told new clothes give women joy, and I'd like to see what you look like... when you're happy."

My heart squeezed painfully, and I couldn't look away from his face, the odd smile still upon his features. He wanted to make me happy. That thought alone made bubbles of joy burst in my chest, and I couldn't hold back a wide smile.

"Thank you, Virgil," I said.

And then, before I could think better of it, I stepped closer, stood on tiptoes, and placed a light kiss on his smooth cheek.

Virgil's eyes flared with light, and he staggered slightly as tendrils of darkness burst out of his chest and reached for me. I gasped, losing my balance, but before I fell, he caught me, his arm supporting my back, and the darkness wrapped around my hands, chest, and stomach.

It felt warm and vibrated gently, like a living body pressed to me. The sensation was completely different from before. No longer terrifying, it was simply pleasant and a bit ticklish. I giggled in surprise.

It felt like holding a purring cat. Even better, like being wrapped in purring cats.

"It tickles," I said with a laugh, looking up at Virgil.

The smile was gone from his face, and his eyes

were dim, only the faintest red flames dancing in their depths. I gasped, my laughter dying on my lips. He looked serious, something intense in the lines of his face and body, and that made me suddenly aware of how close we were.

The side of my body pressed into his stomach and thigh, and his arm around me was firm, his hold inescapable. Not that I wanted to escape. Because the way he pressed me close was so very possessive. Like he truly wanted me.

"I want to kiss you again," he said, his voice quiet. Yet, it seemed to come from more places than one, not just his mouth. The sound flowed from the darkness slithering against my body, and I looked at it worriedly.

"Don't be afraid," Virgil whispered, his voice wrapping around me. "My shadow won't hurt you. It's just another way I can hold you. Feel you."

I breathed out shakily and turned my face up. His eyes were a deep, smoldering red, and a pulse of terror went through me, immediately soothed by the shadowy tendrils brushing over my skin.

"You can kiss me," I said, the words barely audible.

I shook from head to toe, the eerie, uncanny feeling of Virgil's shadow mixing with the excitement of his closeness. I didn't know what it was, what was happening, but my body felt too hot, like a furnace.

Alive and gorgeously warm. Safe. Cocooned in him.

Virgil pressed his lips to mine, and I shivered, opening my mouth with a small sound tearing out of my throat. His arm pressed me even closer, pushing into the small of my back until I arched into him, and he tasted my lips, and then, the inside of my mouth.

I quivered and gasped audibly when Virgil's hard, smooth tongue brushed against mine, gently, as if asking for permission. I gave it, opening to him, and he kissed me deeply while his shadow slid up and down my body, purring tendrils wrapping around my neck, skirting up my scalp, skimming my buttocks and legs.

So sinfully good.

I thought I should protest, because that touch wasn't decent, but I couldn't. My body was out of my control, shaking and burning, completely possessed.

The shadow wrapped around my thighs, and I felt loose and unmoored in its grip. I kissed Virgil back, clumsily yet with hunger that surprised me, and as I moved my lips against his, shyly pressing my tongue into his mouth, everything tightened.

Virgil's arms around me were hard and possessive, his bony fingers splayed wide over my hip and lower back. His shadow pushed against my skin, touching me everywhere, and suddenly, it moved between my thighs.

It slid against the most private, forbidden part of my body, slithering in like a snake, and I jerked, trying to move back. But I was so caught up in Virgil's hold, his shadow wrapped around every piece of me, I couldn't move.

When I cried out to protest, the sound was swallowed by his mouth. Panic rose inside me, a freezing cold terror...

Everything stopped. Virgil's mouth slowly let go of mine, his hands loosened around me, and his shadow unwrapped, running back to him, disappearing inside his body.

One tendril snapped back to the place between Virgil's legs, and I looked away, red with shame.

He stepped aside, giving me plenty of space, and just stood there, looking at me until I stopped shaking, my breath calming slowly.

"You're not running away," he finally said when I breathed out a long, soothing breath and finally looked at him.

"Why would I? You stopped," I said, suddenly wishing he wasn't so far away.

I wanted his comfort. I wanted his touch. But I didn't want to risk him coming too close again.

"I'm sorry, May," he said in that dead, flat voice while his eyes shone blue. "I was carried away. I scared you. It won't happen again."

There it was. Disappointment and relief, two sides of the same coin turning and turning in my chest. I wrung my hands helplessly, suddenly tired from all that excitement.

"It's been a long day," I said, casting my eyes down. "I think I'd like to sleep."

Virgil didn't move or react, just stood there, and I felt a pang of guilt. Hadn't he wanted to watch as I explored my new wardrobe? He wanted to see me happy. But I was deflated and exhausted, and no matter how beautiful my clothes were, I knew I wouldn't muster any joy for them. Not tonight.

"I understand," he finally said. "Sleep well, May."

As he turned away, my heart gave a painful beat, but I ignored it. I went into my bedroom and quietly closed the door.

CHAPTER 9

Virgil

J*ust a bit longer*, I thought, feeling guilty yet unable to turn away.

May was asleep in her bed, and I stood over it, just looking at her. The moon moved as I stayed there, its slow journey across the night sky visible through May's window until it wasn't. Soon, it would be dawn, and I still couldn't be moved from my spot.

My shadow pulsed longingly, but I only allowed it to touch her fingertips. If she woke up and found me standing over her bed like that, she would surely run from me. I couldn't risk it.

And I couldn't risk losing control again. Before, when I had her in my arms, trapped inside me so completely, I could have done anything. I hated to think I could have drunk from her. I did not, but I did something just as bad.

After promising May I would wait until she was comfortable, I couldn't keep from touching her. It was a horrible failing of character on my part.

One ought to keep one's promises. Always.

Especially those given to one's bride.

May moved in her sleep, her face twisting, mouth curving downward. A sound of distress broke out of her, and she twitched, her eyes squeezing tighter, her mouth opening. She gripped the sheets, whimpering, and I understood.

She was having a nightmare.

I stood there, indecisive and conflicted. On the one hand, I shouldn't even be here. I shouldn't see her like this. But I was, I saw, and an overwhelming need to comfort her rushed through me, my shadow jerking and trying to creep closer to soothe May's fear.

Yet, I wavered. Maybe she was dreaming about me. If the nightmare was of me, I would only make it worse by touching her. She might be asleep, but her sleeping mind would know me and go into a frenzy of terror.

Tears streamed from underneath her tight eyelids, a horrible, broken howl tore from her mouth, and I couldn't help it.

I let my shadow do what it wanted, and it pressed lovingly to her hair, smoothing the tense skin over her temples, and poured warmth into her chilled fingers. It surged out of me in waves until it grew large, filling the entire bed frame, and it all wrapped around May, comforting, stroking, giving her warmth.

Such a big shadow. Such a little girl.

She looked so young when she thrashed in her sleep, even though I knew she was nineteen, an adult age for a human. My beautiful bride, all wrapped up in my shadow, as she should be.

May stilled, releasing a slow breath. Her forehead smoothed, her face relaxed, and she returned to peaceful slumber, tension leaving her body.

And even though it did its job, my shadow wouldn't let her go. I stepped back, lowering myself into a plush armchair, and let my darkness wrap around my bride, protecting her from night terrors. Thus joined with her, I let my eyes dim and just felt. The slow rise and fall of her chest. The faint pulse beating in her throat.

The silk of her skin, the tickle of her hair, and her body, fragile, breakable, at my mercy.

It was a sweet torture, one I never wanted to end.

Yet when the sky blushed with the dawn, I left without a sound to catch a few hours of sleep before she woke. My bed felt big, cold, and lonely without her in it.

*

The next few days passed in relative peace. I

accompanied May when she explored the house, learning the quickest routes to her favorite spots. She liked the kitchen, and she often opened cabinets and looked at the food, smelling the bread, opening the honey jars and watching as the viscous, golden sweetness slowly trickled from a spoon back into the jar.

She never ate when I could see, and I allowed her privacy. After all, I wouldn't take her with me when I fed. It seemed fair.

Every day, I battled with the temptation to look closely at her life force. The small flame burning in her chest called to me, its sweet beauty a wonder I wanted to look at for hours, but I held back. May was still weak, and I was afraid I might not be able to resist drinking from her one day.

Tasting her life energy became an obsession, one I quelled ruthlessly, and so I forbade myself from even looking at it. This, while nigh impossible to do, made fighting the temptation easier.

May did her best to adjust to living with me. We spoke every day, we spent many hours together, and she enjoyed everything I provided for her.

Every day, she wore a different dress, choosing those of thick, warm fabrics, covering her shoulders with a shawl or a sweater. My servants made a quick work of adjusting her wardrobe, and soon, all May's clothes fit her beautifully.

Days passed. I didn't kiss her even once, and

she made no move to invite my attention. Yet, I couldn't stop from visiting her bedroom at night. I sat there, in the armchair by her bed, wrapping her in my shadow so completely, she was swathed in it.

She didn't have another nightmare, and I used that to justify my appalling obsession. My presence and touch helped her sleep better. So I continued doing it, even though I knew that if she woke up and saw me, it would be all over.

She would be terrified, and instead of soothing her nightmares, I would become one.

During the day, we took walks in the grounds surrounding my home. They were short at first, just twenty minutes in the garden, but soon, May wanted to venture farther and farther, and I obliged.

I always came with her. I had to steer her clear of my feeding grounds so she wouldn't see the blight my hunger wrought on the land. So she wouldn't fear me.

Every time we came to the fork in the path, I led May left, to the pristine, untouched parts of the woods. They were airier, with birds chattering in the trees, woodpeckers knocking on the bark, squirrels leaping over the ground when they spotted us.

Until one day, May stopped at the fork and deliberately turned right, peering into the gloom under the densely growing coniferous trees.

"What's there?" she asked, and I quickly stepped closer, standing in her way.

"Nothing special," I said. "It's dark. Not well kept. Nobody goes there, and there might be dangerous animals."

Was it a lie? I wondered as we walked under the red-leafed trees, taking the left path, as always.

My hunting grounds weren't beautiful, and that was what I meant by saying they weren't well kept. And if I meant only myself when I said 'nobody', that was true as well. No one but me went that way. And dangerous animals?

A hunter on the prowl was a dangerous animal, indeed.

But I didn't add that I meant myself by this. That the dangerous animal I warned May against lived in the same house as her. That he was her husband in name, and that he spent every night by her bed, watching as she slept while his darkness swallowed her whole.

She couldn't know this. The gift of May's lack of fear was too precious to lose.

Soon, the weather changed, the last golden days of September giving way to the rains of October. The winds grew in power, the air chilled, and the sky was dark with clouds. May preferred to stay indoors, and I had my servants light fires in the rooms she frequented the most.

The kitchen. Her bedroom. The library.

She especially adored the library. Even though the books were written in the language of my home world, May professed to love the sound of it. We spent long evenings sitting by the roaring fire, with her curled at my feet, listening to my voice as I read.

Those evenings brought me comfort. Even though I knew May didn't understand what I read to her, it felt like sharing more of myself with her. I read her my favorite passages of poetry, old romance tales of epic loves and great battles, and as she listened to the cadence and melody of the words, it felt like she understood what I was trying to convey.

You are precious to me. You soothe my loneliness. I will never let you go.

There was one room that May loved even more than the library, which was unfortunate, since it couldn't be well warmed. The ballroom was too big to heat with fire, and it required a throng of bodies filling it to be warm. But even though it was cold and echoing, May visited it every day, drawn to something.

Finally one day, she came to me, blushing and shy, and asked if I could play the piano that stood in the corner of the ballroom.

"Of course," I said, instantly angry with myself for

not showing her earlier. "I also have a violin. When someone lives as long as me, they have no choice but to learn. Come, I'll play music for you."

"Wait," she said, her face hot with a blush. "I'll change into something else. I haven't danced in a long time, but now that no one's forcing me... I miss it."

"You can dance?" I asked, my shadow stirring with hunger. "And somebody... forced you?"

That was new, something that never came up in our conversations before. May didn't speak of her past, and I didn't pry. Yet now that she shared this crumb, I wanted to know more.

"I'll tell you after," she said, her face growing sad. "Right now... I just want to hear music and dance."

Energy buzzed inside me as I waited for her at the bottom of the stairs. I could play music for May. I could watch her dance. And then, she would tell me some of her secrets. All of that combined made me excited, my shadow restless and wanting out.

Soon, May came, socks on her feet, and her dress...

"You're a ballerina," I said without comprehension.

I knew ballet, of course. It was one of the innumerable things my world shared with the human one that my land was transplanted into. Like music and art, ballet was one of the things liches enjoyed the most.

Then. Before the Shift.

"I dance ballet, but I'm not... I am not a professional," May said, casting her eyes down. "It's just that Madame Sundara... the matron... she knew how, so she trained us."

Her mouth curved downward, and she took a deep breath, relaxing her shoulders slowly.

"If I knew ballet still existed in this world, I would have gone to see," I said softly, thinking about my friends who chose eternal sleep over living in this crude, barbaric world.

After the Shift, there was chaos. We didn't realize at once what had happened, because almost all of my country moved between worlds, and liches kept to themselves. When we finally realized something was amiss, because people of various, unfamiliar races passed through our lands, the new order was already established.

This planet that used to be inhabited only by humans was suddenly home to dozens if not hundreds of peoples from other worlds. Each came with large swathes of their land, directly supplanted here. Many humans died during the Shift. Even more—after.

And liches missed it all.

Now, there was anarchy. Each land was ruled by its original race, and humans found themselves without a foothold. They lived in no man's places, inhabiting narrow buffer zones between monster kingdoms. Their cities, cultural artifacts, their art and heritage were mostly gone.

Hundreds of years passed, and the loss still rankled. What I had in my house was what came with me from our world when the Shift happened. Humans lived in my original world, and they made art, music, and wrote books. As did liches. We had a beautiful society, even if sometimes, the beauty was marred by the cruelty of the hunt.

But humans in our world knew what liches were. They revered us, even if their adoration was tinged with fear.

Here, on Alia Terra? There was only mindless terror and disgust, and not just from humans. From everyone.

"We performed," May said quietly. "But men didn't come just to see us dance. Sometimes…"

She broke off, and I saw with alarm, her lower lip trembled.

"How did you get the dress?" I asked, hurrying to change the subject.

"I sketched it," May said, somewhat calmed. "Just for fun. And the next day, I found it in my wardrobe."

"Ah. They took to you. My servants will do that now, so you can use it. If you want something, you can sketch it or describe it. And they will find a way to deliver whatever you want, not just what you need."

May gave me a curious look, and then glanced around, her eyes seeking.

"Who are they?" she asked in a whisper. "Can you see them?"

I shook my head, coming closer, drawn to the fresh openness in her eyes, itching to touch the fabric of her ballerina dress. The cut was different from the ones I saw in the old world, yet still, it was unmistakable. It made me long for my past life of cultured amusement, for the reverence I enjoyed, for how it seemed I could never grow tired and wish for eternal sleep.

I lost so much.

And yet, I gained something, too. She was so very precious.

"I cannot see them, just like you can't," I explained. "My servants are... We used to call them *sussunni*. They are spirits who feed on energy dust. They serve liches because we are the only source of their sustenance. One lich produces copious amounts of energy dust, enough to feed a score of *sussunni*. It's a symbiosis of sorts."

May shuffled a step closer when I spoke, her eyes attentive, and my shadow surged for the surface. I longed to wrap it around her, to draw her close, to drink all her secrets out of her.

"Come. I want to see you dance," I said instead, offering her my arm.

She took it with a smile, and we set off for the ballroom.

CHAPTER 10

May

I *want to dance for him.*
I never understood that before, how some girls wanted to perform when a certain gentleman was present. They danced, giving looks to their chosen spectators, showing their interest. Sometimes, a girl would be selected by her favorite and leave with him at the end of the evening to come back at dawn, looking tired and either happy or very brittle.

None of the gentlemen, as Madame called them, were human, because humans couldn't afford the tickets to our shows.

I usually left right after a performance, shy and unwilling to go with anyone for the night. I knew what happened to the girls who left. They told us about it, some speaking of immense pain, others boasting stories of carnal pleasures and affections.

"He said he would marry me. He said he would take me away. He loves me."

I squeezed Virgil's arm, drawing comfort from his closeness. I hadn't even danced for him, he hadn't known me, and yet, he took me away and married me. I would never hope for love, but I knew how precious everything he gave me was.

And I wanted to dance for him.

The piano's design differed from the old, battered one I knew from the orphanage. In fact, everything in Virgil's home was slightly different from the shapes I was used to. He also possessed objects I didn't know the function of.

And he never tired of showing me around and explaining everything.

All the books in his library were written in the lich language, and I could stare at the beautiful pages for hours, tracing the graceful lines of the letters with my fingers. The paper was thick and creamy, and just handling the books was a surprising pleasure.

My life was awash in pleasures.

But something was missing.

I didn't know how to tell him I was ready, and I hoped the dance would give him the message. After all, that was how the other girls did it.

This was the only way I knew how to attract a gentleman.

"I haven't practiced," I said, blushing with shame when we arrived in the beautiful, spacious room with a high ceiling, a spotless parquet floor, and chandeliers that cast magical prisms on the walls. "It will be very simple."

"It will be a great pleasure," Virgil said softly, and my heart beat harder.

I learned to read him, just a little bit. Now, I could see the delicate, reddish tint at the outer edges of his eyes, and it meant I had his interest and attention.

How did that happen? I still wondered, because just weeks ago, it had seemed impossible I would ever grow comfortable around him, not to mention, want him. But I did. My body thrummed when he was close, and I felt a deep familiarity with him. Sometimes, I longed for his touch, as if it were something I knew and was used to.

On the rare occasions when I saw his shadow, it filled me with awe and longing. I wanted to have it wrapped around me. To be warm, cocooned, safe and wanted. To belong to him completely.

Virgil played an unfamiliar melody, and I stretched, listening closely. It had a strong rhythm and started sweet and light, gradually swelling into a passionate crescendo. As I warmed up my body, I stole glances at Virgil. He played masterfully, his fingers flying over the keys with quick precision, his body moving slightly to the rhythm.

He played beautifully. I wanted to listen to him every day.

The music slowed to a stop, the last, sorrowful note reverberating in the ballroom, and I walked to the center of the room, standing in second position.

"Could you please play it again?" I asked.

Virgil nodded, his eyes a beautiful pinkish orange I'd never seen before, and played.

I began with slow, graceful movements to match the opening music, and Virgil played perfectly, watching my every step.

Soon, the music became more intense, and I quickened my steps, letting every note stream through me. I let go, dancing the way I sometimes did when left alone in the practice room. As I caught Virgil's eye time and again, more red took over until his eyes burned like embers, and I basked in the heat of his gaze.

So that's what it feels like. To dance for somebody.

I pushed myself to the limits, flying through the air, whirling like a thing of wild nature and beauty, hoping my every movement, every step, pleased him. I hoped it would be enough.

I want to stay with you, I told him as I dipped, catching his glowing eye. *I want to be your wife. Make sure I belong to you so you can't turn me away.*

I'm ready. I'm strong enough. I can handle it.

As I danced, I let my fear pour out along with my want, letting go of everything.

Will it hurt? Will you want me? Or maybe you'll think I'm ugly. I tried so hard, Virgil. But I couldn't eat. Couldn't stand the thought you'd turn me away. But maybe if it's done, if I'm yours in every way... Maybe then I can be brave.

I turned and turned, my body starting to hurt from exertion and lack of practice. Sweat stuck to my back, and I turned faster, my socked feet desperately sliding over the smooth floor. I pleaded with him now, letting him see how much I hurt inside.

It's so hard, Virgil. The voices keep screaming, and only you can scare them away.

The music slowed, the final notes playing, and I stopped with my arms stretched high and then took a bow when the last note became an echo.

I stood there, breathing hard, my body hot and soft with all the emotions I let out, and Virgil came to me in slow, graceful steps. His eyes shone a deep red, and there was something predatory in his gait. His shadow was out, like a dark, menacing aura hovering around his shoulders, and I exhaled with relief.

Did he understand?

He stopped right in front of me, the smooth bone

of his face devoid of expression. I took comfort in his eyes, knowing they were full of strong emotions. He felt something for me, I knew that.

"If you don't want me to take you, May, you must leave now," he said in that flat, expressionless voice.

I didn't move.

Virgil's shadow expanded slowly, hovering behind his back like a dark storm cloud, and I released a shaky breath.

"And when you do," he said quietly, "make sure not to run. If you run, I will catch you."

I bit my lip, considering. Would it be better if he caught me? Would it be faster?

Maybe that would be easier. Just make it quick, done and over. And yet, I stayed put. Because I didn't want it to be quick and frenzied. I wanted slow and sensuous, an act I could commit to memory.

I want him, I thought with wonder, a bubble rising in my chest. *Not just so he'll keep me. I truly want him.*

"Please, May. You have to leave," he said, his voice lowered by an octave, coming out dark and menacing as his shadow poured out, snuffing out the light in most of the ballroom.

I watched it with wide eyes, suddenly afraid. I hadn't known it was so big. So very dark. Crackling with something violent... Just like a storm cloud. What would happen when it seized me...?

"Last chance," Virgil whispered, and I tore my eyes away from his Shadow to look at his face.

"I'm still here," I whispered back.

We stood still for one perfect moment. My groom, made of bone and shadow, his body clad in velvet, his darkness filling the room like a brewing storm. And me, a ballerina trembling with fear, ready to be devoured.

The moment broke like a mirror, shattering into glitter when Virgil's shadow dove for me in sync with his arms. He caught me, the roiling darkness pressing to my skin as his arms roamed my back and his lips sought my face.

When he kissed me, my feet left the ground. I gasped, my breath swallowed by his mouth as we were both lifted into the air, weightless like sparrows. As Virgil released my mouth, dragging his smooth, hard lips down my jaw, I glanced down.

We were a few feet above the floor, rotating slowly in a circle, and Virgil's shadow was everywhere. Underneath us, to the sides. As it closed above our heads, cutting off most of the light, I cried out.

"I can't see," I told Virgil, knowing the shadow was half translucent and it let in light. Just not enough for my sick eyes to work.

"Good," he answered. "Close your eyes."

CHAPTER 11

Virgil

I was in a frenzy, but not enough for it to cloud my judgment. I couldn't let May see what I looked like. My face was human enough, but my body was not. Naked, protruding bones, the crackle of energy trapped in my chest where a heart should be, not to mention my manhood— these were all things that would scare her away. Even though I longed to bare myself to her, I feared her rejection just as strongly.

May obeyed me with a sigh, her eyelids fluttering shut, and I returned to her mouth, drinking the sweet flavors of summer from her lips. My shadow caressed her, tendrils wrapping around her wrists and every single finger, racing up her forearms and arms, sinking close to her shoulders, mapping out her spine and back.

She was hot, flushed from the dance and my kisses, and the feel of her, so innocent, airy, and warm like life itself, was a temptation I couldn't resist.

I let my shadow free, and it wrapped around her feet, easily penetrating through the fabric of her socks. It caressed her calves, knees and thighs, her clothes a flimsy barrier that wouldn't keep it away.

May gasped, her body arching, and I pressed my tongue inside her mouth, letting it dance with hers. This was so much better than holding her through the night. She was awake, alive, responsive, letting me do everything I dreamed of.

And yet, I was still wary of touching between her legs, even though I knew her sweet cunt must be hot and alive with a powerful pulse of its own. It entranced me, called to me, and I wanted to touch it, let my shadow explore the inside of it, and then sink into her with my cock, and...

"Virgil, please!" May cried out, and I realized my shadow burrowed under her skin into her arms and legs, pushing inside her body in a frenzy of lust.

I forced it to retreat, dropping small, hard kisses down her throat.

"You didn't like it?" I asked. "Forgive me."

"No," she said, her voice verging on a sob. "I did. It's just... What was it? It was like something was suddenly... in my body... pushing in..."

"My shadow," I confirmed, soothing her with my hands, running them down her back slowly as it heaved with her fast breaths. "It wants to be inside you. It won't hurt you, May. Just wants to be as close as possible."

I knew by now it would not hurt her. Even though I still craved her life force, wanting to devour it just to feel her exquisite taste, my shadow was well trained. All those nights spent wrapped around May's body taught it restraint.

She released a long breath, put her arms around me, and nuzzled her soft cheek into the hard crook of my neck.

"Then let it. I'm ready."

I froze for the briefest moment, shocked by her assent.

Then I let go completely.

My shadow poured into her, pressing inside through her skin and muscle, clinging to her bones. May cried out, and now that I was inside her, I felt her every movement. I felt how she tensed, her entire body taut and filled with kinetic energy. I felt as her toes pointed. As her heart pulsed, faster and faster, and then...

The muscles in her abdomen tensed and released, her body quaking with a powerful force. With my shadow buried deep, I felt her pleasure, the wild, unexpected release, and waves of it crashed through me, making my cock spend itself in my trousers.

I stopped moving, curious what she'd do now. Did she know what just happened? Even I hadn't known she would orgasm from my shadow simply being inside her, wrapped lovingly around her bones and heart.

I didn't even touch her cunt. Not yet.

When she almost stopped shaking, she cleared her throat, and I felt the vibration moving through her trachea. It sent fresh sparkles of pleasure through me. To be so lovingly joined with my wife was exquisite. Something I only read about and thought I would never experience.

Yet, here she was. A beautiful woman who wasn't scared of me against all odds.

"You're happy," she said, her voice filled with awe. "I can... I feel it. You're so very happy."

Was that happiness? It felt devastatingly good and precious, and I didn't remember ever feeling quite like that before.

My shadow moved inside her, caressing her bones, tickling her thrumming heart, racing with her blood through her veins. She cried out, tensing again, and I stopped entirely until she softened with a sob, shaking in my arms.

"It feels... so indecently good," she said, her cheeks hot with a delightful blush. "But I thought... Well, humans do it differently."

She gave me a shy smile, her eyes now open even

though I knew she couldn't see me in the gloom.

"We've barely started, May," I whispered, bidding my shadow to be still so it wouldn't overwhelm her. "The human act is similar to how liches mate."

My shadow stopped moving, coiled inside her so deeply, and just rested, content and fulfilled. I already knew I wouldn't go back to being apart from her. Whenever May was close, my shadow would slide into her.

"Oh," she answered, flustered. "I suppose... I should take off..."

"I will do it," I interrupted, running my hands slowly down her shoulders and arms.

We were still afloat, my shadow creating a field which allowed us to be above the ground, light and unhindered by gravity. As I hooked my fingers under her clothes and slid the skin-tight fabric down her shoulders, she shivered, her body tensing with unease.

I sent a slow pulse of calming energy into her, filling her body with light and peace, and she moaned, relaxing instantly.

"Don't be nervous," I whispered, baring her small breasts and stomach, pushing the fabric down and down, until it floated gently to the floor, and she stood naked in front of me, trembling.

"Don't ever fear me," I said, stroking up her sides with my hands while my shadow slowly uncoiled, filling her body, pressing into every nook and cranny, enveloping her in its loving embrace.

"I will make love to you."

She cried out, trembling when my shadow coursed through her, caressing her from the inside, and my hands went to her breasts, stroking the smooth skin, teasing her. I was never interested in mating, not until I met May. Yet, I studied lovemaking to be prepared for when it happened.

I knew exactly what to do, even if in my eagerness, I was clumsy.

My shadow moved too fast, pressed too hard, and she came again with a delightful cry, falling limp in my arms.

This time, I controlled myself enough not to join her again, but it took effort. My cock twitched and hurt, wanting to spend its release again.

It wanted inside her.

As I held her up with one arm, I pushed my trousers down and off, reassured by the swathes of translucent darkness enveloping us both. She would not see the naked bones in my thighs, the bony scaffolding around them that let my legs appear as if they were human, built strong with muscle.

I shook off my jacket, and since I had no patience to properly unbutton my shirt, I let my shadow slice it to pieces, which fluttered to the floor as I stood naked in front of my beloved, relieved she could not see me.

She wouldn't see the bony expanse of my stomach, hard like a marble sculpture. The intricate scaffolding over the bones of my arms and shoulders, or my protruding ribs.

She wouldn't see my cock.

And even though I wanted to feel her touch, I was afraid she would bolt. The hard curve of my shaft was raised, protruding from my body, its shape like that of a scimitar. The same crackle of energy that beat in my chest now pulsed inside my cock, making it vibrate and tingle with the force of it.

If May touched it, she would feel the powerful pulse of the force flowing through it. Would that send her running? Or maybe other things would.

Like the bony protrusions running the length of it, smooth and hard, like bluntly ended spikes. The low glow bursting out through the cracks in the bony casing, red like the color of my eyes in lust. Or the way it strained, reaching for her, its movements almost prehensile and driven by primal instincts.

To a human, it would appear monstrous and horrifying. Better hide it inside her so she wouldn't see.

"Lie back," I whispered, gently pressing her down. "Don't be afraid, my shadow will hold us up. It's like a cushion. Just lie back on it."

She sighed softly, her body pliant and obedient, and did as I said. I followed her, unable to keep away, and when she rested on the soft cloud floating above the ballroom floor, I was on top of her, leaning on my arms.

Her eyes were closed again, her breathing quick, her cheeks so beautifully flushed.

I let my shadow slowly slither inside her, fanning the flames, and her face contorted as if in pain, and she gave a low moan, squeezing my arms with her hands.

"Virgil, please!"

"Tell me what you want," I whispered, my eagerness almost embarrassing. "I'll do anything, so just tell me."

I couldn't wait to finally be sheathed in her body, but a hint of nervousness held me back.

What if I hurt her? What if she cries? What if I don't know what to do? What if I'm overwhelmed?

"I want you," she said with a sob, opening her eyes and focusing on the glow in my eyes. "Please, Virgil. I'm ready."

Her thighs were open around my hips. I only had to find her opening and notch my cock there, and then thrust. I knew the mechanics of the act. And yet...

"You have me," I whispered, slowly reaching down with my fingers, my shadow buzzing right under my skin, bursting with the need to touch her there. "Shh, May. You have me."

With that, I slowly caressed her between her legs. May bucked and whimpered, and I almost shattered from the pleasure of feeling the pulse of life there. Her sweet cunt crackled with life force the same way my cock did, even if for her, it was more subtle. The susurration of blood, the ample swelling, the inviting wetness... May truly was ready.

I slid my fingers over her hot flesh, and my shadow inched inward, enveloping her entire core with a web of its tendrils. It pressed into the outer parts of her, wrapping the tiniest threads around her pleasure organ, the clitoris.

She cried out and arched, and I stopped moving completely, me and my shadow freezing until she slowly uncoiled. It seemed like my smallest touch brought her to the edge of orgasming, and I had a hard time controlling myself.

To make her shatter over and over again, consumed by pleasure at my hand, became suddenly a lewd fantasy. I would torment her with ecstasy until she fell asleep, exhausted, and then take her freely, without the risk of being seen, of making her afraid...

But not today. Not now.

"I'm sorry," I said, my fingers perfectly still between her thighs, my shadow waiting. "I didn't know it would be so intense for you. I'm trying to hold back, but... It's difficult. You're very beautiful, May. I desire you like I never desired anyone. Completely and utterly."

She sobbed, shaking her head, and then looked into my eyes. I imagined that in the gloom, the glow in my face was the only thing she could see.

"Thank you," she said, her voice hoarse. "I... feel the same way. And don't be sorry, Virgil. It's beautiful. The way you make me feel."

My restraint, already weak, evaporated. I found her opening, positioned my cock carefully, and sank into her.

As she cried out from the invasion, light poured out of my body, the energies gathered inside me so powerful, they needed a way out. The darkness was obliterated, and May's eyes widened when she saw me. All of me.

Gripped by despair, I waited for her to scream.

CHAPTER 12

May

O
h, gods. Oh, dearest gods.
I couldn't move. It was too much, and I could only absorb what I saw and felt, Virgil above and inside me, Virgil, my husband, Virgil—a sculpture.

He was beautiful. I wondered many times what his body looked like, and how closely it resembled human bodies. Was it all like his face, skeletal and yet approximating a human shape? Or was it something else, something freaky that my imagination couldn't even envision?

Was he empty inside his clothes? Was the space just filled with his shadow?

But the reality of him was so much more complex, so delightful. I looked slowly as the light bursting out of him turned to a steady glow and I could see every detail.

I could see the naked bones inside him. There was a wild, roiling light in his chest, red twisting with the darkness of his shadow, like the glow of embers dancing with black smoke. It was behind his ribs. The creamy, proportionate bones protected his chest, a tight armor over his lightning heart, and for a moment, I wondered if I could touch it.

Maybe there was a space wide enough for me to squeeze a finger in. Maybe he'd allow it.

But his heart was only one of the wonders that made up Virgil's body. Because it was like a human one—the shape of it. He filled out his clothes like any man, but instead of skin, muscle and blood, instead of the red wetness of human insides, there was emptiness encased in intricate bony structures.

They emulated the shape of the human body. White, impossibly fragile, they looked like lace.

Virgil was completely still, the glow in his eyes and heart cooling rapidly. I looked up at his face, impassive as always, and wondered what he felt now. He was inside me, we were joined, and my insides beat with a sharp, searing pain that I didn't mind in the least.

I wished I could tell the girls they were wrong. It hurt, but not like being torn apart.

It hurt like being made whole.

"You're…" I began, not knowing how to say what I thought.

All my thoughts and impressions ran through my head, and I felt a bit like dreaming, because it was all so unreal. The ballroom, the shadow keeping us afloat, covering my body in so many tightly wrapped tendrils.

Then it moved, and another sensation crashed into me. Deep, heart-wrenching sorrow. It was Virgil's, and I frowned, trying to understand why he felt that way.

His eyes were back to blue, and he lowered his head, avoiding my gaze. Then he pulled back, making my core clench painfully as he withdrew, and sat on his heels between my open legs.

"Don't go," I gasped, appalled by the emptiness that opened inside me where he had been just a moment ago. "Virgil, please, don't go."

He looked at my face, tilting his head to the side, and I couldn't help looking him up and down again. He was so beautifully proportionate, as if a master sculptor had made him. I couldn't understand how a creature that walked the world could be so perfect.

"Aren't you terrified of me, May?" he asked, and I thought he was surprised. The glow in his eyes turned slightly warmer.

"Of course not," I said, reaching out my hand,

calling him to come closer. "I'm in a bit of pain, I admit, but it's not as bad as the pain of having you gone. Why didn't you... Why have you..."

I blushed, finding it difficult to ask clearly. Asking would involve all kinds of indecent words, and I was never good with them, even when I could think clearly. Now, when my mind was in turmoil, I only stuttered, unable to say what I meant.

"Why I pulled out?" he asked, his head still cocked to the side, the crackle in his chest turning orange. "I thought you might want to run. I didn't intend for you to see me, May. I apologize."

I raised myself on my elbows, even though my body felt achy and sore, and watched him, bewildered.

"But I love seeing you. You're beautiful. Is there something wrong? Do you not like being looked at?"

I knew I didn't, but with Virgil taking care of me, lavishing me with caresses, touches, and pleasure, I didn't even notice when my clothes were gone. Didn't even think about it. Now that I did, though, I blushed and covered my too small breasts, pressing my lips together.

He called me beautiful, I reminded the voices that rose in my head like the buzzing of insects. *He doesn't think I'm ugly. He doesn't!*

Virgil's eyes flared back to red, and his shadow

inside me moved, potent and overwhelming, a bone-deep caress. Suddenly, his sorrow was gone, replaced by a feverish wonder, a kind of excitement that I could not even name, just knew it was like an inferno.

"You love..." Virgil repeated, and I blushed crimson.

I shouldn't have said it quite like that. But it was the truth, and the truth was all I could muster.

My embarrassment evaporated when Virgil surged forward, covering my body with his, and claimed my lips. His kiss was hard, bruising, the marble and bone of him clashing with my teeth, but I didn't push him away.

Even through my closed eyelids, I saw the burning red glow of his desire. Whatever happened, it seemed to be all right now, and my body trembled with anticipation.

There would be pain. But... He would fill my emptiness. That made it worth it.

Virgil pulled back, and his lips hovered over mine, so close. I wrapped my arms around him, trying to hold on in case he wanted to leave me again. But all he did was nuzzle his cheek against mine, his eyes dimming for a moment.

"You are so precious to me," he whispered. "The most beautiful creature in the world. And you belong to me. You're all mine. I don't know if I can believe it, May."

"I'll prove it to you every day," I said, feeling his tender awe reverberating inside me, moved by it to tears.

He really felt this way about me.

"I wish I could make it not hurt," he whispered in between dropping kisses over my face and head. "I'm so sorry. But I'll do my best."

"Please, be inside me," I said, too overcome with want to be ashamed. "I need you."

Virgil's shadow moved through me, slow and deliberate. It warmed my limbs and fingers, made my insides pulse with a relaxing glow of pleasure, until I moaned at how exquisite it felt. Like being submerged in a hot bath, filled with warm milk, completely satisfied... Only better.

I was deeply aware of Virgil above me, his legs between mine, his face nuzzling over my cheek, kissing me reverently. As his shadow pulsed in me, leisurely and so warm, Virgil positioned himself between my legs again.

My breath stuttered in apprehension, and then, his shadow pooled low in my belly, filling the entire space between my hips, pulsing in slow, ungodly pleasure.

I cried out as my muscles loosened and warmed, fresh blood pouring in, the tension replaced by almost pain. My body expanded, filling up and swelling, making more space in its suddenly relaxed state.

Virgil pushed inside me, and this time, the pain was barely there, and it was so very easy. So natural.

I was like warm, soft butter, and he was a knife.

And then my insides coiled in pleasure, tensing and gripping. He felt hard inside me, and too big, forcing my body open, making it receive him. I felt the slide of him against me, my muscles squeezing him tight, enveloping him. I closed my eyes, hissing when he pushed further in, deeper than I thought possible, and just tried to feel him.

But other things called my attention. The emotion pulsing through me with the beat of Virgil's shadow, and it was a profound awe, devotion, more things I could not even name that swelled in my chest and made me want to weep, because I didn't know how else to express them.

His loving mouth on mine, pressing gentle, soothing kisses into my lips. The way his body hovered over me, so protective, strong, and beautiful.

"Shh, my darling," Virgil whispered, growing still inside me. "You're doing so well, my sweetest. Does it hurt? I will wait a moment. Give you time."

"It doesn't," I replied, and it was the truth.

He filled me in a way that was both blissful and

uncomfortable, but the pain was gone, replaced by a hot, hungry pulse.

"You are so brave, so very good for me," he whispered again, dropping kisses along my hairline. "It feels numinous to be inside you. I never thought... But it is. I want to worship you. I want to never leave. I want to always be in you, so close, so warm and alive... Oh, May. You're making me babble like a fool. I can't contain it."

"I want to hear everything you have to say," I said, opening my eyes and looking into his. "It's beautiful. Everything you say and do. I love it."

Virgil shook his head, a flash of lightning suddenly bursting out of him in a blinding wave. I squeezed my eyes shut, and at that moment, Virgil thrust into me with force until I cried out.

I didn't realize he had more to give me. And now, he pressed so close, his hips nestled between my legs, and it seemed like he was completely buried inside me. So full. So deep.

"Have I hurt you, sweetest?" he asked, dropping frenzied kisses over my face. "Shh, my treasure. It's done. There is only pleasure after this. I'll give you time. I can't wait, but for you, I'll do anything."

I panted in fast, gulping breaths, trying to calm my quivering body, but it proved impossible. Having him so deep inside me, being full of his shadow and him, made me feel like I was insane. My body shook and wanted, my mind tumbled through waves of sensation, and all I knew was that it was too much for me to handle and that I never wanted it to end.

"Please," I begged him. "I need... This is too much."

"What do you need, sweetest?"

I shook my head violently, because I didn't know. I just wanted this pressure inside me, this horrible, wonderful tension, to ease or crest.

"I need you... I want..." I sobbed helplessly, not knowing how to tell him.

"Hush, my love. I know. I'm here. I'll help you."

And as Virgil slowly pulled back, moving inside me in a way that made sparks explode between my legs, his shadow surged and crashed through me, filling me with bliss, pouring in and in until my pleasure peaked and broke, streaming through my body in potent waves.

I blinked my eyes open, instantly drawn into the red glow of Virgil's.

"There, my sweetest. All better."

And then he moved, his hips working, and the relief I felt dissipated as another bout of tension started to build.

CHAPTER 13

Virgil

It was so easy, after all. My body knew exactly what to do.

I moved inside May, loving her with my cock, and even though it wanted to spend inside her already, I slowed down every time it came close and waited, forcing the tension inside me to relax. Being in May like this, with her legs wrapped around my back, her arms on me, her sweet cries filling the air, was too exquisite to let it end.

By gods, I could spend an eternity like this. I'd never succumb to eternal sleep now that I had her. I would never give this up.

May mewled and writhed helplessly under me, her trembling legs squeezing me tightly, and I moved faster, letting my shadow bring her to another peak. As it did, her face twisted in an expression of torturous bliss, her sweet cunt gripping me tight. Loving me back.

I still couldn't believe it was real. She saw me and wasn't afraid. She wanted me. Gave me herself, something no one had ever done. It made the energies in my body frenzied with possessive joy and lust, and so I moved inside her, stopping when it seemed like I would come, and then brought her to orgasm when it seemed she couldn't stand it.

But soon, it became too hard to control myself. My shadow was restless, moving through her even when she was relaxed and easy after coming, and then, my hips would not stop.

They pushed back and forth, my cock moving easily inside her now that it stretched her open. She trembled and begged with small sounds, and as I felt the powerful pleasure gripping my lower back, flashing through my shadow, the tension reaching into all parts of my being, I made her come one last time as I poured my release deep into her body.

The ecstasy gripped me, my shadow slipping out of control, and we were flung higher, stopping right under the ceiling, our joined bodies turning and turning, May on top, me on top, May on top...

As her cries quietened and my pleasure poured out, my life force bleeding into the ballroom and through the walls, we gently floated to the ground with me below her. I wasn't soft to lie on, but I was warm, and I wanted her to be on top of me, not the cold floor.

We rested. I lay there, my treasure in my arms, my energies subdued and content. And May... My shadow caressed her slowly, reaching for her mind until I realized she was asleep.

I let her sleep. There was no need to move, to do anything. All I wanted was to be inside my wife, my cock and shadow buried in her. It was perfection, pure happiness and light, and I never wanted it to end.

She woke hours later. As she stirred, making a sleepy sound, I caressed her back, soothing her in her transition from slumber to waking.

"Shh, my love," I whispered, stroking her head. "My wife. I have you. Everything is good. It's almost dawn, and it will be a sunny day. The sky is red in the east. Good morning, my love."

May tensed and then exhaled slowly, moving her hips until my cock slipped out. She gasped and froze, her face red, and I stroked her more urgently, determined to soothe all her discomforts.

"What is it, sweetest? What's wrong?"

May shook her head and looked at my face, raising herself slowly on shaking arms.

"Hello, Virgil," she said in a hoarse, lovely voice that instantly reminded me of the sounds she made last night. My cock, which was eager all the time it spent inside her, pulsed with a new crackle of energy, ready to love her again.

"It's morning already? And I slept... with you?" she asked, looking away as her blush deepened, giving her cheeks a lovely color of life and rushing blood.

"Yes. You were with me all night. I held you," I said.

My shadow, eager to say its own greetings, slowly uncoiled inside her, caressing her from the inside.

Her eyes widened, and she collapsed on top of me with a low moan.

"Virgil," she said, her voice breathless. "But we shouldn't. If it's already morning... Oh!"

"Why, my love? I want you all the time. Night, morning, afternoon, evening... As long as you're able, I want to have you at each time of the day."

"Oh," she said, hiding her face in the crook of my neck. "I... But I'm sore..."

My hands stilled, and my shadow quivered with shame.

"Forgive me," I said, loosening my hold on her. "I was selfish. I'm so sorry, May. Though it's hard not to be selfish now that I finally have you."

I slowly untangled my shadow from her, unwrapping it tendril by tendril from her skin first. I made it pull out of her sweet cunt, letting go of her core completely as it slithered back to me. She shivered and moaned, arching her back, and I whispered words of comfort.

"I'm sorry... I should have let go when you slept

but couldn't bear the thought of parting from you. Forgive me. It's almost done. You'll be free in a moment. Shh, my sweetest. It's almost done."

She sobbed, and my chest squeezed with anger at myself. I was too eager, too intense, giving her so much more than she could handle. I should have controlled myself better. But she made it so difficult to hold back, I was frenzied. Even now, it took so much effort to pull away...

"No," May breathed, nuzzling into the crook of my neck. "I... Not yet. I want to, now. M-make love to me, Virgil."

And just like that, my control was obliterated. I let my shadow surge back in, claiming her from the inside, making it lift us both up, and rolling us in the air until I was on top of her.

She cried out from the force of my assault, and when her cunt still spasmed from the orgasm my clumsy eagerness caused, I thrust into her, my bliss pouring out as blinding gold light.

It was quick this time. I couldn't hold back, so I thrust in her sweet body, making her come two more times before my own release came. I loved the way she gripped me tightly when she orgasmed. It felt like being wanted and craved. Like belonging.

Here she was, my lovely wife, forever mine.

After I was done loving her with my shadow and

my cock, I carried her to the bathroom and drew her a bath. I washed her, bathing her body in foam and washing off her sweat with warm water. Then I carried her to my bed and took a bath myself. When I returned, she was sleeping.

I didn't feel tired, even though I hadn't slept. Instead, my senses were sharper than ever. My instincts, which clouded my judgment before, were finally satisfied. My mind was clear. Unbiased.

And so, when I lay next to her, something nagged at me, a sense of unease. I embraced her slowly, and she didn't even stir in her sleep. I pressed my shadow all around her, burrowing into her body... And there it was.

Something I didn't notice before, because I trained myself not to look at it too much. Because I did my best to resist the temptation, to protect my beautiful mate from myself. Now, with my instincts sated and my gaze sharp, I could see it clearly, and the realization poured aghast terror into me.

Her life force. It was much too faint. Too weak.

Almost extinguished.

With a cold panic, I thought for a moment that I must have drunk from her. I must have taken some of her life, and my wife, who had so little to give, suffered because of it.

I lay with her, and when my mind calmed somewhat, I analyzed everything that happened last night. With relief, I realized I didn't feed at all. In fact, I spent exorbitant amounts of my life force, and I was almost depleted. I had to hunt soon.

When my frantic fear slowly calmed, reason taking over, I realized I would have remembered drinking from her. That experience would have eclipsed even the pleasure of mating.

Then why was she so weak?

And then I knew.

She was ill. Or, maybe she didn't get enough sustenance. I cursed myself, angry for taking her when she still wasn't strong enough. When she still wasn't recovered.

And yet, she spent weeks in my home. By all rights, she should have gotten stronger. There was enough food, I knew. She took regular mealtimes, even though I wasn't present for them.

She should be better. So why wasn't she?

I prodded and searched with my shadow, examining her life force from every angle, but it gave no signs of illness. Just weakening. Her flame was dying from lack of fuel.

Which meant I needed to feed her. Desperately.

I called my servants and ordered them to prepare a meal for May. Bread, honey, milk, boiled eggs, thin slices of ham, pumpkin cakes. We got all that during our last visit to town, and she was so happy picking out her food.

I thought she was eating. But maybe not enough.

When the tray arrived, I woke her as gently as I could, though without lenience. May moaned and shook her head, and still, I made her sit up in bed and placed the tray in her lap, bringing the cup of warm milk to her lips.

"Drink, my love."

She took a few sips and then grimaced, turning her face away. I put a spoon in her hand and pointed at the assortment of foods.

"Eat whatever you want. But you must eat enough for the flame inside you to be stronger. If you don't, you could die. And I won't let you."

May gave me a startled look and picked up a currant bun, nibbling on crumbs she slowly tore away. I sat by her side patiently, watching the small globe of her life force. It did not grow stronger.

"If this is not to your liking, have something else," I said after a quarter of an hour passed, and not even a half of the bun was gone.

"I'm tired," May said, looking away. "Leave the tray. I'll sleep and eat later."

"You will eat now."

She startled, her wide eyes going to my face.

I knew I spoke sternly, and she watched me with a guarded expression, something in her eyes flickering. My shadow, still coiled inside her, told me what it was.

Fear.

For the first time since we met, my wife was truly afraid of me.

I recoiled, wanting to call my words off, wanting to apologize and take it all back. After the boundless joy and pleasure of last night, after experiencing her being so open and generous, that fear was like a cut. It hurt, and my pain flared through me, extinguishing my flame for a moment.

She gasped.

"Your eyes... They are black."

I shook my head and forced myself to calm down. This wasn't about me and my fears. It was about my wife and the meager flame that burned inside her. Something was eating away at it, and if I didn't do anything, she would be gone.

I gave in with a sense of finality. Her being afraid of me was the most agonizing, impossible torture I could imagine. And yet, I would gladly bear this burden if it meant May was healthy and well.

So there it was. I was so infinitely selfish, I would force my wife to live at all costs. Because I couldn't be without her.

"Don't mind my eyes. It happens sometimes," I

said. "Eat, May. You must. If you don't, the energy inside you will go out. You'll die."

She shook her head, tears springing to her eyes.

"But I'm not hungry," she whined, her fear whipping into a frenzy with a strange kind of despair.

"It doesn't matter," I said, not letting my voice grow softer, even though my chest hurt to make her feel like this. "You must eat, because I refuse to lose you. I told you I was selfish. This is what it means. I will keep you and make sure you're well and healthy. Even if I have to hurt you to achieve it."

Her eyes widened, and she tensed, watching me with surprise. And then...

My shadow felt it happen and recoiled instinctively, feeling her pain. Something inside May cracked, and she burst into tears, sobbing wildly. I took the tray from her lap and sat next to her, taking her in my arms.

"Shh, my darling. Don't worry. I will take care of everything. You only need to tell me what's wrong."

CHAPTER 14

May

I cried and cried, shaking in Virgil's arms. I couldn't bear showing him my shame, my weakness. I would rather die than disappoint him.

Couldn't he see that the very fact he cared was the cause of my weakness?

I didn't defeat the voices, after all. They ruled me and told me what to do, now more than ever.

Because Virgil had called me beautiful, and I didn't want him to think I wasn't. I didn't want to change. To lose his affection and admiration.

And so I worked to remain beautiful the only way I knew how. By eating less and less every day.

There you go, Madam Sundara's voice soothed my frantic thoughts. *You're almost there, May. Almost a butterfly.*

Except... didn't Virgil say I was dying? Was that

what it meant to turn from a larva into a butterfly?

To die?

"I'm sorry!" I sobbed out, taking comfort from his patient embrace. "I was stupid, but I can't... It's the only way I know how to be beautiful."

Virgil stroked down my hair and back, his shadow caressing me gently from within until I felt stronger, and my sobs subsided. Only then did he reply.

"What way?"

"Not eating," I said, twisting my face away. "That's how... How one creates a body that's pleasing for men. For dancing."

It was the truth. Of course, it was. Yet, I knew it was just the outermost facet of the truth. The least repulsive part of it. I couldn't show Virgil the rest, and I hoped desperately he'd be appeased by this shallow truth alone.

He was silent for a long while, just holding me gently and stroking my body with his hard, warm hands. I breathed almost calmly, doing my best not to let the smell of the food get to me. It was true I wasn't hungry, because my body did not feel hunger anymore. And yet, the idea of stuffing myself full was a constant presence in my mind, taunting and pervasive.

Finally, Virgil spoke, and I focused on his words to keep my mind off the food. Yet, his words stung like a slap.

"There are no men here for you to please," he said, and through his shadow, I sensed his anger. It made me shake. "There is only me, and the way to please me is different. I have told you already. I wish for you to be healthy and thriving. I want your life force to be powerful and robust. May, I have told you this. So who is this man you're trying to please? Because it is not me."

I shook, fresh tears spilling out. He was being unfair! I was doing my best, trying my hardest, but the voices... They wouldn't let me rest. They never stopped. And they kept calling me ugly. Unworthy of his love. A disgusting larva that just wouldn't transform, no matter what was done for it.

"I'm trying!" I cried out, willing him to see. "I tried to eat! I did! Three meals a day, no matter how long it took, but... But it was so difficult. And you... I didn't care as much at first. You were a stranger. But you were so good for me, so sweet, and we spent hours together every day, and I... I started to care. And it became impossible to eat. I want to be beautiful for you!"

Virgil stroked my hair lovingly and for a moment, he said nothing. And when he spoke next, he kept touching me soothingly, even though his words hurt.

"So you care for me, and that is why you want to die? This is what I understood from what you just said, and it makes me angry with you. It also hurts. I've never been hurt because of another person's words, May. It's a quaint kind of pain. It feels like only you can soothe it."

I swallowed through my tight throat, a headache pounding in my temples. This wasn't about him, not really, but I made it sound like it was. I didn't even understand myself, and my thoughts were getting jumbled.

I just wanted him to go away.

"I'm sorry. I didn't mean to hurt you, I'm just so tired. Please let me sleep!" I begged him

"No," Virgil said, pressing his cheek to my hair. "I want you to tell me why you don't eat. I considered the reasons you gave me and they don't make much sense."

Suddenly, I was no longer tired. I was livid. My heart beating in a feverish rhythm, I tore myself out of Virgil's embrace and faced him, breathing hard.

"Don't pretend you understand me!" I said, my voice verging on a sob. "You're not human! You don't have a head full of voices that scream at you at every step! You say you've been hurt by words for the first time? The words in my head cut me every day until I'm bleeding!"

I watched him, breathing hard and just daring him to fight me. But Virgil cocked his head to the side, his eyes dimming until they were dark blue, and asked, "What do the voices say?"

I hesitated, but I came this far. I might as well tell him everything. It wasn't like he could find me any uglier. Any more disgusting.

All was lost.

Keeping my sobs trapped in my throat, I told him, the venom that usually accompanied the words slipping out of my throat, poisonous and harsh.

"You're fat and lazy, May. You think anyone will want you if you stay like this? Such a disgusting, repulsive girl with her gob full of food. No wonder your parents left you. They couldn't bear looking at your pudgy face, you pig. They couldn't love you, and no one should blame them. If you don't try harder, nobody ever will. Stop eating! You look so pathetic with your cheeks full of lard. You must try harder, May. Don't be a disappointment. You think men want to watch fat ballerinas? Such a lazy girl. You'll fast until you lose ten pounds. Maybe that will teach you something. Maybe once you see how beautiful you can be, you'll learn."

After I spat out the vile accusations circling in my head, I fell back on the bed, exhausted and empty.

Virgil's shadow wrapped around me, tightening around my heart, and I didn't protest. I lay there with my eyes open and unfocused, breathing quick, shallow breaths, my heart fluttering like a butterfly in a trap. And it really felt like it. Like I was about to transform, only now, it terrified me.

"Am I really dying?" I whispered.

"No. I won't let you."

I wanted to laugh, but my body felt feverish and weird, as if I was detached from it. There was a pain in my chest, and I swallowed with difficulty. Now that the anger was gone, only weakness remained.

"Time to go," Virgil said softly, scooping me off the bed.

He carried me in his arms, and through the fog poisoning my thoughts, a dull heartache penetrated.

So this was it. Like everyone before him, Virgil was going to reject me. He would pack me up into his carriage and send me away.

I shook, sobbing soundlessly, and wished I was stronger. More beautiful. I wished I was a woman who could be a butterfly without dying.

"Shh, my dearest," he soothed me, his shadow sliding over my cheeks and collarbones with sweet tenderness as he stopped in front of the wardrobe in my room. "It's not far. You'll be well again. I told you, I won't let you die."

"You... You're not letting me go?" I asked, confused by his words.

"Never," Virgil said, his shadow tightening. "I'm

sorry, May. You're about to see something truly ugly, something that will make you fear me, and I still won't let you go. Now get dressed so you don't freeze out there."

Virgil turned politely away, letting me get dressed, but when my fingers shook, he turned back and fastened the buttons of my dress for me. Next, he dropped to his knees to tie my shoe laces. When I was dressed, he picked me up again.

He walked out of the house and turned onto the path to the woods surrounding his estate. I rocked gently with every step, and his shadow kept moving through me, coiling and uncoiling anxiously.

Worry and determination pulsed through it, into me, and I grew unsettled, wondering what Virgil planned.

"I thought it was fair," he said, briskly following the path. "Since I didn't show you how I fed, not letting you see my feeding grounds, I thought it was only fair not to watch while you ate. I understood your discomfort. At least, I thought I did. But May, there is nothing displeasing about the way you eat. Indeed, it would give me great joy to see you take the food I provide for you. I would be happy to see you grow stronger for me."

I pressed my lips together, keeping quiet. I knew he was sincere, and it troubled me, because what Virgil said clashed so strongly with what I was taught.

No man worth having wants to see a woman eat and grow fat.

Was Virgil not worth having? No, it was wrong. Virgil was the only man—lich—being I wanted, and I longed to please him in any way I could.

But the thought he might watch me eat and enjoy it made my skin crawl with unease. It didn't feel right. Even worse, it seemed like a lie.

"I was a coward, May," he continued, his voice flat as always, his eyes cool. "I hid from you, and I let you hide from me until you almost faded. My cowardice almost killed you. So now, I will be brave. I will show you how I feed, then I'll feed you from the life I hunt down, and then, you'll have a choice."

A cold wind rustled in the red and brown leaves in the trees, and I shivered until Virgil's shadow coiled more tightly around me, keeping me warm. But his embrace couldn't stop the fear that took root in my heart.

I'll feed you from the life I hunt down...

"What does it mean?" I thought, shivering. "Will you feed me... raw meat?"

I gagged just thinking about it.

"It won't be bloody," he said, and somehow, that made it worse. "About the choice you'll have, May. You can refuse to eat after this. I will feed you instead. And you will come with me every time and watch how it happens, because you have to know the price."

He stopped at the place where three paths crossed. The one behind us led back to the manor. The one on the left was the one we always took when we were out walking. And the one on the right...

It was the path I wanted to explore earlier, but never could. Virgil always found a reason to steer me away from it, and I obeyed, even though curiosity lingered.

Thick fir-like trees grew on each side of the path, making it look dark and eerie. I shivered, wondering again why Virgil never wanted to take me there.

But it seemed I wouldn't have to wonder for long. He turned and slowly walked down the right path, his eyes turning yellow.

"And if I manage to do what I intend and terrify you so thoroughly, you'll never want to look at me again," he said quietly, his shadow withdrawing from inside me and making it impossible to discern his feelings. "You'll choose normal food. You will decide you never want to see this again, never want to be a part of something so dark and ugly. You'll eat human food out of terror."

I shook my head faintly, thinking that surely, Virgil would never do anything so terrible that I would fear him so much. But as the darkness thickened, the firs muffling the sounds until we were enveloped in thick, cold quietness, I hesitated.

Could he really be so terrible…?

CHAPTER 15

Virgil

I walked fast, steeling my resolve. The will to turn back and find another way rattled in my chest, but I knew there was no time. May had to be fed, and there was only one way to do it.

By feeding her the life force from another being like her.

I usually sustained myself using energy from trees. It lasted longer and was less volatile when consumed. It would do nothing, however, to make up for the damages May did to her body. The energy from trees, if I transferred it to her, would extend May's lifespan, but only if she were well enough.

Which was why I had to hunt.

The dark coniferous trees, the cover hiding my feeding grounds, soon petered out revealing the destruction I wrought on the land.

May gasped, freezing in my arms, and I nodded once. With the trees ahead of us naked and the October sun high in the sky, albeit hidden behind silvery clouds, she saw everything.

This was the reason I withdrew my shadow from inside her. I didn't want to experience her disgust firsthand. Just seeing it etched on her face was bad enough.

For now, though, May wasn't terrified or terribly upset. Mostly, she looked around with wide eyes, her lips parted.

Ahead of us, the ground dipped, forming a valley. We stood at the edge of it, overlooking it whole. The valley was a place of death.

All the trees were naked and blackened, their bark peeling in places, some of their branches dry and dead, breaking. They looked old and wizened, but frail. Not like mature trees that had lived to old age. These were often small, young trees, taken by death too early.

"Some will be reborn in spring," I said quietly, unable to stand May's resounding silence as I took the path down the gentle slope. "I take care to leave enough so I can feed again next year. But soon, I'll have to switch to the other side for a few years. Let this part of the woods recover."

The undergrowth on each side of the path was blackened and withered, but deeper in the dead woods, it looked normal, some bushes still holding wild fruit. On the ground, mushrooms grew, flashing with brown or yellow, sporting small bite marks.

I walked quietly now, May's shallow breaths the only sound. The wind blew in my face, which meant hunting would be easy. Even with May's human scent clinging to me, I wouldn't startle the game unless it heard or saw me.

"I leave enough for the animals to stay," I whispered. "They have food and water in the nearby stream, and since the trees look a bit like in winter, the landscape doesn't scare them. In fact, being so exposed, they are less flighty than animals living under thick canopies. You'll see."

May shook her head weakly, and I quickened my step. She had little time left. And I... I had to stop putting off the inevitable. The trees were bad enough, I knew, but to see me hunting would terrify May for good. I feared it like I never feared anything.

Yet, it had to be done.

A branch snapped ahead of us, and I let my shadow rush ahead, thin, translucent tendrils flying silently through the air. I walked faster, scouting with my shadow, until I sensed the prey.

A young fawn. So young, it might not survive the winter. It must have been born too late.

I scouted for the mother, but she was nowhere

around. Good. I only needed the young today.

When my shadow reached the small deer, I gripped it in one strike, tightening the coils around its legs and body, keeping it secure and unable to run. It thrashed, panicking, and May stirred in my arms, hearing the sounds.

"You need to be fed from the same kind of energy that fuels you," I said, doing my best to explain.

Even when I knew she would see me as a disgusting monster, I still held hope. Maybe she would understand. Maybe, one day, she would forgive me for what I was.

"And it's better when it's young. There is so much more life force in a young being. All those years, all the potential stored inside, ripe for the taking. You won't have to eat for months after this, May, and you'll still thrive."

"But what..." May started, breaking off when we turned a bend.

There it was, the fawn my shadow had bound. It waited by the side of the path, subdued and trembling, looking up at us with its big, wet eyes.

"No," May whispered, shaking just like the youngling. "No, Virgil, you can't... It's a baby!"

"I'm sorry," I said, unrelenting. "You'll die if I don't feed you. I explained. If you want to avoid this in the future, you only have to start eating, May. But today, this is necessary."

The fawn shook, twisting its thin neck to look up as I approached. Its fur was a soft brown, its back dappled, everything perfectly shaped. It was healthy, its life force had a strong current, and now I couldn't even pretend it would have died in winter.

It might have lived. But I wasn't going to let it.

"No, Virgil, please!" May shouted when I sent more tendrils to wrap around the fawn, swathing it in my shadow so completely, so soothingly, it relaxed. "I'll eat! I promise, I will! Whatever you tell me to, I will do it, just don't...."

I slowly lifted the fawn off the ground, its eyes closed, its quick breaths calming slightly. It was suspended in front of us, swathed in my darkness. I braced myself and pierced May's chest with my shadow, making her cough and whine like a hurt animal.

"I'm sorry," I said one last time, already mourning everything we had together. "It's the only way."

And then, I drank. The fawn was asleep, comforted by my mind-controlling magic, so it didn't feel a thing. But May saw and felt it all, because she had to. I refused to feed her covertly. She had to be aware of the price.

The little deer's life energy, all those years stored in its body, bled through me into May, and as they did, the animal shrunk and shriveled. For a moment, there was a ghost of the doe it might once have been, proud and strong, but it dissipated as energy bled from the fawn.

It took maybe a minute, and when I was done, only a frail, crumbling skeleton remained, covered with stripes of blackened fur.

In my arms, May thrashed and shook, her starved body receiving the deer's energy. She cried out in pain as her cells, used to operating on so little, suddenly received so much fuel. Her heart strengthened and pumped with a renewed vigor, her mind was set ablaze with a rush of power, and the flame in her chest grew robust and heated, the way it was supposed to be.

She grew heavier in my arms, more substantial, her body recovering. The fawn's remaining six years of life would be greatly reduced, since so much of that energy was spent on May's body rebuilding itself, but she would still have long months in which she wouldn't have to eat.

And then... We'd do it again. Unless I terrified her so much, she would now eat without complaint.

When it was done, I slowly lowered the deer to the ground and covered its body with fallen branches, my shadow doing the work. May was still in my arms, gulping deep breaths that expanded her chest, shaking and moaning. Her body was in shock, and I did my best to soothe her, pouring calmness and warmth into her, but not too much.

I didn't want to cloud her mind or confuse her.

She had to be aware. She had to feel and remember everything that happened.

When she stilled, sobbing quietly, I turned and walked slowly back home. My shadow wasn't inside her any longer, because I was not that strong. I couldn't bear the pain of her rejection.

When we reached the fork in the path, she gasped softly and gripped my jacket.

"I can walk. Please, let me go."

Keeping my gaze averted to prolong the moment before I had to face her disgust, I lowered her to the ground. She stood in front of me, and I looked at her body, avoiding her face. Her fists were clenched, and she didn't shiver despite the cold.

So in that, at least, I succeeded. May was well. She'd live.

"Is that how you eat?" she asked, her voice ringing strong, too. I couldn't discern the emotion in it, but there was something there. Most likely anger.

"Not usually," I said, still not looking at her face. "I feed from trees. I am not an animal, so I don't need animal energy to survive. I prefer plants."

"Have you ever done this to people?" she asked again, and there was such despair in her voice, I couldn't help but look up.

Her eyes glistened, her skin glowed, and even her hair, so thin and lifeless before, was lush and healthy. And there was no disgust in her face. Just fear and anger.

Her cheeks and lips were red.

Pain squeezed my chest as I beheld my wife, who I knew would never touch me now. Never dance for me. Never give me another timid smile.

I traded her love for her life.

"Yes," I answered, seeing no need to hide anything now. "Back home... Before the Shift, that is... I fed from humans. Usually not too much. It was... ah, a delicacy. And the human beings in our world revered us. For them, it was a great honor to be chosen as a lich's offering. I haven't fed from any people in this world, though. They fear me enough as it is."

She blinked, shaking her head, and then looked up, seeming confused.

"The Shift was hundreds of years ago. And you talk about it as if you remember it."

"I do. I was there when it happened."

She shook her head again and then hid her face in her hands. Her shoulders shook, and a pain bloomed in my chest. I knew she suffered, and it was all because of me.

"I'm sorry, May."

Her hands fell away, and she looked at me with such loathing, I had no doubt as to what she felt.

She hated me.

"I want to be alone."

I shook my head, my shadow twitching, eager to reach for her and wrap around her so tightly, she'd never be able to leave.

"I won't let you go," I said, watching her steadily despite the hate in her eyes. "I'm sorry."

May's nostrils flared, and she shook her head violently, sending her hair flying.

"I'm your wife," she said with quiet vehemence. "I made a vow, Virgil, and I won't try to run. I just need to be alone right now."

We looked at each other for a long while until I finally nodded and turned away. As I walked back to the house, I thought I no longer had a reason to watch her. She saw the worst. I could let her wander my grounds without a worry, her promise good enough for me.

I trusted her.

So when darkness fell, and she still didn't return, her betrayal was tenfold as painful. May lied to me. She promised she would stay, and yet...

She was gone.

CHAPTER 16

May

I watched his retreating back with a mixture of conflicting emotions. What Virgil did... What he was...

You knew, a quiet voice in the back of my head whispered, *ever since those two women in town tried to get you to run from him, you knew.*

They didn't tell me much, because Virgil was back before I could ask any questions. They told me he was a lich, a species that was undead. They said he'd hurt me. *Suck me dry.*

But I married him, for better or for worse, and at the time, I felt safe with him. He made me warm. He cared for me. The vague, unnamed fears the women tried to instill in me didn't take root, because I was all alone and just wanted to belong.

He was the only one who wanted to keep me.

I grew to love him with time. And last night, I

was so in love, so happy. He made love to me, and I loved him back, and it was the most beautiful experience of my life.

Today, he killed a baby deer and made me watch, and then he forced the animal's life into me, making me well.

Gods help me, I thought with shame. *Gods help me, but I can't hate him for that.*

I couldn't. Virgil made it plain he did what he did to save my life. I knew he was right. I was dying. If I was honest with myself, I would have acknowledged the signs much earlier, and maybe then, today's tragedy wouldn't have happened.

It was my fault.

I shook my head, frowning as I walked slowly in the direction of Virgil's hunting grounds. Should I blame myself? I tried to be good. I truly tried. But the voices... They punished me for every bite of food, made me hurt until all my defenses crumbled, and I could only listen helplessly and believe they spoke the truth.

But there were moments, coming more and more often the longer I lived with Virgil, when I was almost free. When I woke up in the mornings, well rested, warm, and happy, the voices didn't speak. Only later during the day they would wake and start nagging.

When I was with Virgil, they mostly remained

silent. Maybe they feared him. Or maybe he made me stronger.

Should I have told him sooner? About the voices? Could he have helped me?

Sometimes it felt as if there was someone else in my head, in my body. A menacing, harsh-eyed presence whose only purpose was to hurt me. I didn't want it there. It was like a demon, one I didn't know how to exorcize.

I walked fast, dead leaves crunching under the soles of my shoes. My breath rushed out of me in small clouds of heat, and I marveled at how fast I could walk, how strong I felt. I was warm, and something powerful and comforting hummed in my chest, in my bones.

It was life, power, fuel. A fire that burned within me, making me feel as if I could run and run, and not stop. As if I could take on the world.

I wasn't a butterfly, that was certain, but I didn't feel like a larva, either. I was a deer, I thought, cringing when the memory of the wide-eyed, trembling fawn emerged in my mind.

I was a doe, running on strong legs, breathing in the fresh forest air. I was a doe, and the price for my life and health was another life, and it couldn't be undone.

But I could prevent this from happening ever again.

I stopped under the naked boughs of a tall tree, looking up to see a raven watching me with its beady eyes. I breathed fast, tired after the exertion, yet oddly elated as my heart beat strong in my chest.

I wondered why Virgil's power seemed like such a perversion.

Humans hunted animals. Indeed, most races did. Orcs, trolls, shifters, minotaurs... They all hunted for meat. So why was I so shaken by the fawn's death?

Because most don't kill the young.

Hunters killed for meat. That was why they left the young and females alone. A big buck would feed many more people than a fawn. But was it more moral to kill an adult animal than a young one? Virgil didn't hunt for meat but for their life force. So instead of killing one young fawn, he could have killed two adult bucks, and gotten the same amount of energy...

My head spun, and I sighed, setting off again. I didn't know what to think, so I decided not to judge Virgil at all. He had to eat, like every creature. And he said he usually chose trees and took care not to take too much... The entire forest was his pantry, and he took care of it.

I couldn't judge him.

One thing I could do was eat properly. And I would.

I felt so much stronger now, as if with physical health, my mind got healthier as well. I was alone in my head, not even one poisonous whisper marring my thoughts, and maybe, if Virgil helped me... Maybe I could stay well.

With that hopeful thought, I reached the place where the baby deer who gave its life for me lay.

It was quiet, not a soul nearby, and I dropped to my knees by the small, shrunken body and just looked, facing that horror again.

Blackened fur, black just like the bark of the surrounding trees. It was like rot, or like the absence of color. When Virgil devoured life, did he also drink the color? I would have to ask him.

The fawn was clearly a desiccated corpse, and I sighed deeply, not even a trace of a smell lingering. A clean death.

"I'm sorry," I whispered, bowing my head. "I wish it didn't happen."

And then, because a sacrifice like that couldn't go unacknowledged, I lowered my head even more.

"Thank you," I whispered. "Thank you for saving my life."

A few minutes later, I was on my way back to the house, thinking about what I would tell Virgil. *Everything* was the right answer, and even though physically, I was strong enough, I was still afraid. He wasn't letting me go, that was clear, but he could think less of me, and that was a terrifying thought.

Please, don't be disappointed.

I reached the fork in the path and turned back to the house when a sudden rustle made me stop.

"Miss! Miss!"

Someone was in the bushes, whispering as loudly as they could. I looked around, but I was the only person on the path.

"You mean... me?" I asked, taking a tentative step closer. "Who are you?"

"Be quiet, miss! We're here to save you, we are. Come closer, and we'll hide you. You can come with us."

I frowned and shook my head, remaining where I stood.

"What do you mean, save me? I'm fine."

And even as I said that, the image of the fawn being slowly sucked dry of life flashed in my mind, a terrible memory that I knew would return in my nightmares.

"You're in danger!" the voice answered, urging.

I stepped closer, noticing movement behind the thick evergreen bushes. Another voice joined the first, this one clearly female and not bothering to whisper.

"He's messed with her head. Liches can do that,

you know. Come on."

A moment later, three people, two men and a woman whom I vaguely recognized from my shopping visits to town, rushed out from behind the large bush. Before I realized what was happening, one man grabbed me while the other clamped his hand over my mouth. The woman produced a rope.

I struggled and fought, my muffled screams much too quiet to reach Virgil. And despite my new strength, I was weaker than my attackers. They tied me up and gagged me in no time, and soon, I was carried away down the path to a cart waiting beyond the bend.

"It will wear off in a few hours," the woman said, brushing my hair off my face. I glared at her, trying to growl, and she tsked at me. "You will thank me yet, missy. When you come to your right mind, you will thank us for saving you from that demon."

I shook my head and struggled harder, panic creeping in when the cart rode briskly, jostling on the uneven path.

She had it all wrong. Virgil wasn't a demon—he was the one saving me from the demons in my head who tried to kill me. Why were these people doing this? Virgil was my husband. I belonged with him.

When we were far enough from the manor, the

woman loosened my gag. I screamed for Virgil instantly, my throat hurting from how loud I was, but the woman only shook her head with pity.

"Virgil, eh? That's a pretty name for a monster. Save your breath, missy. He won't hear you."

"He's my husband!" I spat, trying to get to my knees, which proved difficult with my hands tied behind my back and the cart jostling hard. "Let me go! I want to be with my husband!"

The woman gave me a disapproving, slightly disgusted look, and shifted away when I fell back to the bottom of the cart with a grunt. It was no use getting up. But I needed to get free. I promised Virgil I'd stay.

"Husband," the woman sneered, the look of pity flickering out of her eyes as she gave me a hard stare. "I hope for your own sake you didn't lie with the beast. Nothing good would come of that, mark my words."

I wanted to scream in her face that indeed, I did lay with Virgil, and that he made the most beautiful love to me, but before I could, one of the men spat over the side of the cart and turned toward us.

"If she lay with the lich, better throw her in the river. What if his spawn is inside her? It will bring a curse on us all, you mark my words. Everything will rot and die. You better throw her somewhere she won't be getting out of."

I shook my head, suddenly afraid. His *spawn*? Did they mean... if I were pregnant? I couldn't be. I hadn't bled in a year...

And yet, if Virgil healed everything in my body today, there was a small, tiny chance my womb was well, too. And if that was the case...

"Well, have you?" the woman asked, peering at me angrily. "Better speak the truth!"

"Never," I answered, doing my best to protect myself and the little seed that could be growing inside me. "He doesn't... Liches don't do that. Only living men can... you know."

I blushed as I said it, but the woman seemed satisfied, and one of the men gave a loud hoot, pumping his fist.

"Damn straight, they can't! No heart to pump that blood, eh? Well then, girly. Maybe you'll get a proper husband in town, see? One who can get it up!"

He laughed raucously, and I breathed a sigh of relief. I didn't know how much they knew about liches, but clearly, not enough. I was safe from being drowned, at least.

An hour later, we arrived in town, and I was put under lock and key in the mayor's house. I was kept alone in the room until sundown, when the woman who captured me returned, bearing a cup of milk and a piece of bread. I refused the food, and she shrugged and ate it herself.

"This is the only town that has a mayor, you know," she said after a while, pride in her voice. "Other towns, the monsters rule there. But we have a human mayor. You're really lucky to be here. You'll have a good life, you'll see. We just need to wait till your head clears. Not long now."

I held back a sneer, understanding finally why this town prospered and why the people were so defiant. It was because liches didn't rule like other monsters did. I didn't even know if there were other liches. Just Virgil. And he kept to himself, barely leaving his house to do shopping.

And when he was out, they treated him with deference, clearly afraid. But when he was away... They got cheeky.

If I still had this energy later, if I dealt with all my issues and became strong like I wanted to be —a doe, not a butterfly—I would put this town in order. I didn't know yet how, but it irked me so much they would think badly of Virgil when he did nothing to hurt them.

I remembered the shifters that ruled our town. Humans by day, beasts by night. It was their fault everyone was so poor and Madame Sundara's business thrived.

I couldn't imagine Virgil coming to her establishment and participating in what happened there after a performance. He would ask questions, try to make things right. Or leave, at least.

But those monsters? They never left.

The ungrateful townsfolk here had no idea how lucky they were to have Virgil.

I had to get free, get better, and... do something. I wasn't sure what, but the energy thrumming within me longed to be directed into action.

"I think I feel better already," I said, doing my best to look sincere. "This really is a beautiful town."

The woman nodded, satisfied, and looked at me hesitantly, tapping her chin with her finger.

"We'll wait a bit longer. Just to make sure."

"Thank you," I said, remembering what she said in the cart. That I would be grateful once my head cleared. "Thank you so much! You were so good to me, took such a risk... Thank you for bringing me here."

I only needed her to unbind my hands and let me out. Just that. And once she did, I would run back to Virgil.

The woman nodded with satisfaction, motioning for me to turn so she could free my hands... As she cut the ropes, it turned out I wouldn't have to run to Virgil, after all.

He came for me.

A loud, terrifying voice boomed outside the

mayor's house, shaking the glass in the windows. "Give me back my wife!"

CHAPTER 17

Virgil

My shadow knew her, and so I followed her trail, sorrow, anger, and the pain of betrayal flaring in my chest and urging me on. That May would promise her fidelity and then leave me was like a hammer crushing my bones, the deep ache reverberating in my entire being.

I trusted her. Indeed, I loved her. She was my reason for everything.

And now, she was gone.

But I would get her back. May was my wife, and the marriage was consummated. According to the temple's rules, she had a duty to stay by my side forever unless I mistreated or hurt her, and that I did not. I would never hurt her.

She was mine by all laws and rights, and I would drag her back no matter how much she screamed or fought.

I stopped in front of the mayor's house, a beautiful structure that mimicked some architectural details of my home, and I let my shadow out. The humans gathered in the market square made noises of fear, and a moment later, the town militia burst out from behind the house, bearing lit torches and clumsily made guns. I ignored them.

"Give me back my wife!"

I let my shadow pour out and out, drinking the light from the nearest street lamps until half of the square was dark. The ranks of militia shuffled, and a young, roundly shaped man stepped forward, bearing the town's flag.

Blue with a sunflower, it was a pretty thing, one I sometimes suspected was a symbol of their love for life and hate for me.

"We don't want you here, lich!" he screamed, and though his voice was strong, the flag in his hand shook lightly. "Go away from our lands and never return!"

My shadow shot for the man, and before the militia realized what was happening, I had him in my grip, raising the portly body over the cobbles, squeezing so hard, he could barely breathe.

With shouts of fear, the men dropped their weapons, one going off with a loud bang, and scattered, pathetic and helpless against the power they didn't understand.

Everything in me whirled in a violent frenzy. May was still in that building, and for whatever reason, she wouldn't come out. My shadow reached for the door, readying to shatter it into splinters, when the man in my grip wiggled, moaning, and suddenly, all that frenzy and anger turned into a craving.

Here he was, in my grasp, brimming with life. Ripe for the taking. It was so very long since I sampled human life force, and having May right under my nose and denying myself for those long weeks was excruciating. There was no reason to hold back with him, though, was there?

These people defied me. They hid my love away from me, helped her betray me. They feared me and plotted behind my back, even though I never even touched them. Why should I hold back?

"You took my wife from me," I said quietly, slowly raising the man higher and higher while the militia watched, wide-eyed and shaking a distance away. "You took my dearest treasure, hid what's mine, and you think I won't punish you?"

I squeezed harder, depriving the man of his breath. There was a satisfying snap, a rib breaking, and he opened his mouth to scream, but with no air, there was no sound. I pressed harder, ready to plunge my shadow right into his frenetic heart...

"Virgil! Virgil, stop! I'm here! I'm here! Virgil, please, take me home!"

I dropped the man and turned, all of my shadow

rushing for May. It gripped her and brought her close, crawling over every inch of her body, pushing in to rest under her skin, wrapping around her heart. I was restless, hungry, half-relieved, half-hurting.

"Why did you leave?" I asked, embracing her tightly with my arms, and she sobbed, shaking, overwhelmed by my shadow's assault.

But I couldn't stop. I thought I lost her. I thought she was gone, that she left me, and now she was here, back in my arms... If only to stop me from slaughtering the humans.

Was she only here for this reason? To protect the humans? To choose them over me?

I froze, that thought making me mad with fury, until my shadow found raw, reddened skin on her wrists. It pressed closer, healing the abrasions until she moaned, her eyes fluttering closed. And I knew, the understanding pouring into me like an ocean of relief.

They tied her up. She didn't come willingly. She didn't leave me.

I sagged against her, happy and heartbroken all at once, cradling my wife in my hungry arms. She was here. She was mine. She didn't leave me.

"What happened?" I asked while a crowd gathered around us.

The militia, the town-dwellers, the mayor with

his family…all stood around us, watching, keeping their distance and hating us. And I didn't care what they thought of me, but May, my sweet May? I would not allow them to look at her with unfriendly eyes.

Not when she was so vulnerable, shaking in my arms. Not ever.

I poured my shadow out, spanning it wider and wider around us. There were gasps in the crowd, and the spectators moved back in a rush until I forced them into narrow alleys, and the square around us was almost empty.

"They tied me up," May sobbed, clinging to me. "Oh Virgil, they thought you controlled my mind. They thought they were saving me. And I begged them to let me go, but they wouldn't until I lied and now… you are here."

I pressed her closer, as close as I dared with people watching, and looked up, cold wrath brewing in my chest.

"Give me those who took my wife."

My voice was quiet, and yet, the crowd gathered in the alleys rippled, my message clearly heard. There were gasps, whispers, shuffles. I held May, soothing her with my shadow, running my hands down her head and shoulders, reassuring myself she was by my side.

When I tired of waiting, I made my shadow rise

above me like a pair of terrible wings, and asked again.

"If they don't stand in front of me within a minute, I will walk into every house in this town and take one life from each as punishment for what you did."

Cries and wails broke out in the crowd, and May gasped, extricating herself from my hold.

"Virgil, you can't! They are stupid and they did wrong, but you can't kill them!"

I cocked my head to the side, my anger so powerful, it made me see the world in shades of red and purple.

"Why not? It's what they expect of me."

Just then, three people stumbled out onto the square, clearly pushed out from the crowd. They started running, heading for the houses, and I seized them all with my shadow, making them dangle above the ground.

"Did these people take you, May?" I asked, watching the ruddy, terrified faces of two men and a woman.

"Yes," she said, her voice verging on a sob. "But please, don't kill them!"

I squeezed all three, letting my shadow inch closer and closer to their hearts, pushing it down their throats so they couldn't breathe or scream.

"They took you, May," I said, curbing my urge to take revenge so I could listen to her.

It was difficult. I just wanted to crush those who dared to touch her. Yet, if she begged for their lives, I had to listen, at least.

"They did," she said, taking my face in her hands, her frantic eyes searching mine. "And everyone here expects you to kill them, because that's how they see you. But I don't! I know you are kind, careful, and generous. I know you only take lives to sustain yourself. You don't kill to make others live in terror."

"They live in terror, anyway," I said, wavering.

May's voice burrowed inside my chest, reaching the inferno within. As she spoke, the taste of revenge suddenly soured in my mouth, and yet, I didn't let go.

"They don't!" she said. "They only think they do. But Virgil, this town is flourishing. I've seen other human dwellings, and they are nothing like this. These people prosper because of you. Please, don't break it now. Please? For me?"

All will to crush and destroy whooshed out of me. I loosened my shadow's grip and put May's captors on the ground. But I couldn't leave them unpunished.

"My wife pleaded for your life," I said, while the three coughed and squirmed, still in my hold, but free to breathe and stand. "But I can't let you go freely. I want it to be clear: anyone who so much as looks at my wife the wrong way, who speaks unkindly to her or touches her with the intent to harm, will be punished."

The crowd was now closer, lining the houses surrounding the square, so many terrified eyes trained on us. May said they prospered, and indeed, they did. They grew so confident, they thought they could take my wife to lure me out and defy me with their meager militia ranks.

It was time to do something about this town. If not for me, then for May.

"These three people are to be banished," I said. "If I see or sense them in this town tomorrow, or any day after, they will be killed, no matter how much my wife begs me. Because no one is allowed to touch her. No one is allowed to take her from me."

There were gasps, cries, and one of the men fell to his knees, hiding his face in his hands. I continued.

"Anyone who doesn't like living on my lands is free to leave, as well," I added after a moment. "Because this town belongs to me. Some of you live in the houses that were built by people who revered me. Who built this town because they wanted to be close to me. They made music, art, wrote beautiful poetry to please me, and that was why I allowed them to stay."

May shivered in my arms, watching me with

wide eyes, and there was a hush over the crowd, punctuated only with the sobs the banished man.

"But you? You are ungrateful. You look at me with fear and disgust, you plot how to drive me out, you dare to capture my wife!"

My voice grew loud with anger, and I pressed May closer, my shadow slithering deeper under her skin to help me stay calm.

"There will be changes," I said, knowing what I had to do so this would never happen again.

It was time to take on the mantle of a ruler. Even though these people seemed hopeless, even though they were so different from those who lived here in my home world, I had to try. For May.

"You will prepare a festival, like the people in my lands did before the Shift. You will line up singers and performers, prepare hot foods and drinks, raise stalls and organize entertainment for the children. A month from now, it will all be ready, and me and my wife will be your guests of honor."

There were whispers, but the crowd remained mostly quiet. I suspected they were surprised by my demand.

"And if the entertainment you provide pleases me, I will bestow gifts."

A few surprised cries and voices rose, and I heard a child talking excitedly, the word 'gifts' like a magical spell, turning their fear around.

"It will be a festival of gratitude. This town is mine. Everyone who lives here belongs to me. I give you protection from other races, I give you freedom to develop and prosper, I keep your woods clear of wild beasts. For all that, you should be grateful.

"If you don't wish to be a part of my people, living under my protection, you are free to leave. But if you stay, know that I will demand loyalty and obedience. I will not forgive defiance or betrayal."

The crowd was quiet, and a cold wind blew over the square, making May shiver against me. I tightened my shadow's hold around her and stroked down her back.

"If you are loyal and do as I say, if you treat my wife and me with the respect we are due, you will be rewarded," I said. "This is the way it was in my land before the Shift. And this is how it will be now if you allow it. Now, go home. I will return later to see if the three traitors left as I ordered. Good night."

And with that, I picked up my wife and carried her home. With the sweet weight of her in my arms, the burden of having to deal with the humans in town didn't seem as heavy. Indeed, I was mildly excited about the changes I could bring. The world I could build for my wife and our future offspring.

But there was something else driving me to go faster, exciting me far more than any plans of ruling. My wife was back in my arms, and I was eager to remind her to whom she belonged.

"Tonight, I won't let you sleep, my love," I said quietly, my shadow slithering lightly along the skin of her legs when we left the town behind. "You are mine. I'll do everything in my might to show you."

CHAPTER 18

May

Virgil carried me the entire way back. On foot, it took him over an hour to get there with me in his arms. Once we were home, he drew me a bath and bid me to get in.

I blushed, pressing my hands to my clothed chest, and Virgil simply watched me with red-tinted eyes, patient in the brightly lit bathroom.

I knew I was naked with him only this morning. But it wasn't so light then. And the air didn't shimmer with such incredible tension as it did now.

"Can I wash on my own?" I asked, nervous about showing him my body under the bright lights.

"No," Virgil said, taking a step closer. "I need you, May. I need to see you're mine. Today... It hurt, my love. It hurt so much when I thought you left me."

That confession was no less moving when spoken

in Virgil's expressionless voice. Tears sprang to my eyes, and I undressed without a fuss, shedding all clothes and then forcing my hands to remain at my sides despite an urge to cover myself.

For a moment, we just stood opposite each other, and Virgil watched me with deep red eyes, his head moving as he appraised me from head to toes and back. I blushed furiously but set my mouth in a line, braving his open gaze.

If he needed me to stand naked in front of him to soothe his hurting heart, then by gods, I would. No matter how much it cost me.

"You're so beautiful, May," he said, slowly coming closer. "My exquisite wife. The beautiful energy strumming in your chest, flowing through your veins, is irresistible. I adore your body, but the power flowing within you is what I love the most."

I shivered when Virgil stood opposite me, his hands slowly running up my sides to cup my breasts. His eyes dimmed, and he tilted his head back, slowly caressing my skin until a sound escaped me, a soft whimper.

His eyes brightened, and he let his shadow loose, wrapping me in it until I couldn't see myself. A moment later, I felt the familiar prickling when it burrowed under my skin, pushing deeper and deeper in, wrapping around my bones, filling my breasts from the inside…

My legs buckled, and Virgil caught me in his

arms and lowered me into the bathtub full of warm water. He sat on its edge, and his shadow poured out, dozens of dark, moving tendrils, some thinner, some thicker. They poised above the water, all trained on me.

"Virgil..." I gasped when his shadow moved within me, a slow, languorous wave that rolled through me from my feet to my head, carrying with it a charge of dark, insurmountable pleasure.

"You belong to me," he whispered, his red eyes watching me relentlessly. "And I take care of what's mine."

His shadow descended, pouring over my skin, wrapping around my toes and fingertips and higher up, claiming my forearms and arms, encasing my legs wholly, surrounding my hips. It stroked my skin, massaging, and Virgil watched as I slowly unraveled, shaking from pleasure and the overwhelming, delightful touch.

The tension and fear of the day were washed away with the shadow's persistent caresses, dissolving in water. But then, a new tension built inside me, something thirsty and desperate, and I whimpered and thrashed as his shadow moved through me, too slow to give me a release, yet too fast to let me feel anything but the obscene, indecent presence of him inside my body.

"Open your mouth," Virgil whispered among the sounds of splashing water my body made when fighting the pleasure. "Let me in."

I obeyed, and his shadow filled my mouth with its dark warmth. It tasted like nothing I knew, pure movement and energy, and it caressed me from the inside, shadowy tendrils dancing with my tongue...

It was a kiss.

"Open your legs," he whispered, and in the delirium I was in, in the echoing chamber of the bathroom, his voice grew big, commanding, enveloping me from all sides just like his shadow did.

With a moan of surrender, I obeyed, and shadowy fingers caressed my inner thighs, reaching higher and higher, until they poured inside me, penetrating my body.

I cried out and heaved, bucking in the water, but the shadow's arms tightened around me, holding me still while it filled me with sinful pleasure. I couldn't hold back the moans and screams, couldn't resist its attack, and ecstasy poured through me whole, reverberating in my body, pulsing through my flesh and bones.

It was bliss, utter and decadent, and it lasted for so long, my mind grew dark, my body heavy, my thoughts scattering like sparrows taking flight. I was broken, shattered into pieces, only the dark beat of him within me holding me whole.

"Beautiful," Virgil whispered, reaching with his hand to brush wet hair off my forehead. "This is how I want to see you, May. Every day. Mine to take. Mine to please. Mine to take care of."

My eyelids were heavy and my heart frantic when he took me out of the water, strong, smooth arms curving around my body with possessive certainty. It seemed his pain was soothed, his suffering wiped away, and I burrowed my face in the crook of his neck with a relieved sigh.

"Thank you, Virgil," I whispered when he carried me to his bed, candles flickering to life as we passed them. "You came for me and brought me back. That... I don't think you know how much that means. No one in my life, no one before you, would have gone after me if I got lost. No one did. That was why I lived in the orphanage. Because I got lost in a crowd when I was five years old, and my parents didn't look hard enough to find me."

I shook, pressing my face to his bony neck. I was ashamed. Even after all these years, confessing how unwanted I was filled me with the fire of shame.

"Maybe they didn't even look at all," I whispered. "Maybe they were glad I was gone."

Virgil sat down on the bed, arranging me more comfortably in his lap. I was in his arms, cradled like a child, and his eyes turned back to blue, all the red of desire going out of them.

"Is this what you were told?" he asked, his shadow purring within me, a comfortable warmth spreading from where it was coiled around my heart.

I looked away, unable to bear the unreadable flame of his gaze.

"Yes," I whispered. "I don't remember much. Just that...there was a crowd. I think people were screaming, and running, and my mother's hand slipped out of mine. I tried to look for her, but everyone was so big around me, and everyone was running, and there were loud noises... And sometimes..."

I broke off, sighing deeply and wondering if he would scold me for telling him my fantasy the same way Madame Sundara did. But Virgil stroked my cheek with his fingers, his shadow humming inside me softly, and I gave in.

I could tell him. Even if he thought I was wrong, he would be kind when saying so.

"Madame Sundara told me my parents lost me on purpose and forgot about me as soon as I was out of their sight. She said I was ridiculous for believing otherwise... But sometimes I imagine it was different. All those shouts, the running, the chaos I remember... I wonder if maybe they wanted to look for me but were hurt. Maybe people were running from danger. Maybe my parents were hurt looking for me. Maybe that's why they never found me. Because they couldn't."

When he hoisted me up and brought his lips to my temple, I cringed inwardly, awaiting his verdict. I wasn't brave enough to believe this fantasy on my own, not when it was crushed so thoroughly by the matron. But if Virgil said it was possible, maybe this deep shame and pain inside me could be laid to rest.

"This is the only explanation that makes sense, May," he said softly, stroking my hair. "I can't imagine someone did not look for you when you were gone. You are the most precious treasure in the world. Of course your parents looked for you. If they didn't find you, it means they are dead, because only death could keep them from getting you back. I'm sorry, my sweetest. They must have loved you very much."

I cried and cried in his arms, and he held me patiently as years of hurt and rejection poured out of me with bitter tears. Virgil soothed me with loving caresses but let me grieve as long as I needed, until a gray dawn lightened the sky, and I still shook with sobs, rocking gently in his warm embrace.

"I'm sorry," I whispered when the tears ended, and I couldn't cry any longer. "I know you had other plans for last night, and I..."

"May." Virgil interrupted me sternly, turning the blue flame of his eyes on my face. "Don't apologize to me. I am here for you. I am yours, just as you are mine, and I only want this: to be with you, to take care of you, to hold you through your pain and through your joy. I want your everything, even the parts you're ashamed of, even those you think are ugly. To me, you are perfect."

His words launched more tears, and I sobbed. But even though my stomach hurt from crying all night long, even though I was tired, my face swollen, I finally felt whole. Virgil letting me cry, staying with me through my pain, was the most beautiful gift he could have given me.

When I cried out everything, I felt calm and empty in a way I never felt. I was hollow, and in the places made empty by the tears, Virgil's shadow took root, curling up like a cat in my chest.

"I'm sorry if this is hard for you," he said when it was completely light out, and I just lay in his arms, staring without focus at his bedroom and the candle flames, now pale in the morning light. "But we will both have breakfast before I let you sleep."

I waited for the voices to rise, spewing their poison and making me nauseous at the very thought of eating, but it was quiet in my head. The hollowness inside me was in my mind, too, vast hallways of thought that used to be busy and crowded, now empty. I pressed closer to Virgil, laying my palm over his chest, and sighed deeply.

"It's okay. Will you… Will you eat, too?"

The memory of the dead fawn emerged from the calm depths of my mind, causing a flicker of sorrow and grief, now muted in my exhausted state.

"Yes. I thought it might be easier for you if we did this together. But I eat mostly plants, May. It shouldn't be grisly. At least, I hope it won't."

I sat up by his side, sensing rather than hearing the uncertainty in his voice. He hid that from me, I remembered. He said he deliberately didn't show me how he ate before I forced his hand.

It was my turn to comfort him.

"Thank you for saving my life," I said simply, cupping his hard cheek with my hand, brushing my fingers over the smooth, warm bone. "It was terrible but necessary. I understand that. And I'm sorry. I know it was hard for you."

Virgil didn't answer, only held me in his arms, pressing his face to my hair. Soon, the door opened, and a tray of food flew in and hovered by my side until I straightened and it settled in my lap.

While I got a sweet bun with honey and jam, a small cup of sweet cheese, a bowl of late raspberries, and a glass of warm milk, what settled in Virgil's lap was a...

"Potted plant?" I asked, too astounded to laugh yet. "Are you really going to... Oh."

He looked at me with those blue, glowing eyes and gave me a smile, that creepy, unnatural expression that looked like he didn't truly know what a smile was.

I smiled back, though, and laughed softly under my breath, because the domestic coziness of that moment filled me with such a glowing warmth, it could only be happiness.

"We can dine outside when it's warmer," he said, ducking his head as if in embarrassment. "But while it's cold, I thought this might be preferable."

"Is it some kind of herb?" I asked, lowering my head to smell the delicate leaves that spread away from thin, spindly branches, a silver sheen coating the smaller ones. "It smells so fresh. Like rosemary and something else..."

"It's an herb from my lands," he said, gently pushing my head away. "Breakfast, May. The sooner we're done, the sooner you can sleep."

"I'm not sleepy," I muttered, facing my tray.

Because even though the voices were quiet, my old habits were so deeply rooted, even the thought of eating with Virgil by my side filled me with unease. I looked at him, his eyes trained on me, the potted plant held firmly in his hands, and I sighed.

He was uncomfortable, too. He was brave for me. So I could be brave for him.

I picked up the bun and took a bite, chewing

fast to keep myself from thinking and worrying. I followed it up with a spoonful of the cheese, popped a few raspberries in my mouth, took a sip of milk…

And the faster I ate, the easier it became, until my stomach was full, and I looked up with a grimace. Would I ever get used to that feeling?

But the sight of Virgil distracted me from my discomfort. His eyes were dimmed and his shadow, dusted with silver, was wrapped around the plant. Slowly, it withered, the leaves falling and drying so much, they turned to dust. Soon, nothing remained of the plant, only an empty pot full of black soil.

Virgil's eyes brightened when he looked at my tray. I ate over half of my food and drank the entire glass of milk, and he nodded, putting the pot away.

"Are you still not sleepy?"

I yawned, the food in my stomach making me groggy, and Virgil nodded again, gesturing to my tray. His invisible servants whisked it off my lap, and he tucked me in, smoothing my hair and kissing my temple.

"Sleep, and I'll feed you from my shadow so you can live forever by my side."

As I drifted away, my nostrils filled with the herbal scent of the plant Virgil consumed, making me smile against the pillow.

CHAPTER 19

Virgil

The sun slowly dipped below the horizon, and I watched its progress through the uncovered window. I slept with my body pressed to May's back, my shadow entangled in her so thoroughly, I doubted I'd ever manage to pull it away.

Now, I was awake, my cock stirring, teased by her closeness. But she was tired, and she needed to sleep, so I waited, content just holding her, keeping vigil over her sleep without having to hide my presence.

She was naked, and her uncovered, rosy breast moved slowly with her every breath. I undressed before joining her in bed, and her warm, satin skin felt luxurious against my bare body.

Finally, she stirred, whimpering softly in her sleep, and I sent a calming wave through her, chasing away any nightmares that might plague her. But May whimpered again, pressing into me, and I realized with wonder she wasn't having a nightmare.

Her body wanted me, even in sleep.

"Shh, my sweetest," I said, stroking her hip and gently plucking her rosy nipple. "I'm here. I'll answer all your needs."

She sighed, her hips moving against me, her mouth open. I played with her nipple, uncoiling my shadow so it could fill her from within, and May cried out, her eyes flashing open.

"Too fast," I said. "I'm sorry, my love. I wanted to let you sleep longer."

"Sleep...?"

She turned in my arms, watching me dazedly, until her cheeks colored, and she pressed her lips together.

"Don't be embarrassed," I said, kissing the corner of her tight mouth. "Your body wanted me, May. I tried to soothe your need."

She whimpered, her cheeks growing hotter, and I peppered her forehead and temples with kisses, my hands roaming her body along with my shadow. Soon, she closed her eyes and uncoiled, embarrassment leaving her as pleasure coursed through her freely.

"Just like this, my sweetest," I said, caressing her breast and side, moving down to slide my fingers up her hip, kissing down her neck, just over her pulse. "Allow me to take care of you. I will give you everything you need. I will soothe all your wants."

We were tangled together under the sheets, warm and intimately close. Soon, May grew restless, her hands exploring my body, and for a moment, I froze, wondering how she would react.

But then, she pressed her hot core to my thigh and moved back and forth, making sounds of pleasure, and I understood my wife truly wanted my body. Not just in sleep, but in waking, too.

I let my shadow bourgeon within her, caressing her between her legs, moving through her with force until she cried out and spasmed in pleasure. I didn't stop. I did it again until she sobbed, shaking, her body tight, coiled, wave after wave of bliss pouring through her.

And I did it again.

Her voice grew hoarse, her nails clawed over me, and she still gripped my thigh between her legs, moving against it deliriously until I pressed closer, harder, my shadow claiming her whole, and she fell apart with a wild howl.

"Is this how much you need me, my love?" I whispered, soothing her skin with soft caresses while I built another wave within her, unable to help myself.

Having this power over my wife's body, being

able to bring her to orgasm over and over, was exhilarating. In my selfish heart of hearts, I wanted to hook her, make her reliant on me for her pleasure, for her needs, for her everything. Because I was never letting her go.

"Please... Virgil... Oh!"

She peaked again, and I watched with wonder how hard her heart worked, how hot her cunt was, how much glowing, delicious energy coursed through her. A flood, insurmountable, so great maybe I could take just a little sip... Just a taste...

"May I taste you?" I asked, my eyes flickering with excitement. "Please, May. Just a little bit. I won't hurt you, I promise. Just the tiniest bite..."

"Yes!" she cried out. "Anything!"

My shadow was already deep within her, and I pushed it to where she was the hottest, where her energy pulsed the most. I filled her cunt to the brim and pierced deeper, connecting to the current running through her and drank, and drank, and drank...

She cried out, spasming again, and I tore away, orgasming as her taste streamed through me, delightful, overwhelming, May's life force as sublime as life itself. I buried my face in her hair and shook, the beauty and wonder of her filling me with profound emotions I couldn't understand.

We both shook in each other's arms until May's

breathing calmed, and she stroked down my cheek with trembling fingers. Then, she brought her hand under the covers, hesitantly, and it brushed against my cock as she slid her fingers up her stomach, where I spent my release.

"I apologize," I said, my voice unsteady. "I shouldn't have, but I couldn't resist. Just tasting you alone… It was the purest bliss."

She pulled her hand out and looked at her fingers, her eyes glassy and hooded, her lips parted.

"It glitters," she said, fascinated. "Did you know that?"

My eyes dimmed in embarrassment as I shook my head, watching her fingers critically.

"I'll carry you to the bathroom, so you can… May! What are you doing?"

She brought her fingers closer to her lips, and I caught her wrist, worried.

"You tasted me," she said, avoiding my eyes as her cheeks flamed. "I think it's only fair."

She brought her hand closer to her mouth, and while I didn't let go, I didn't hold her hand back. Instead, I watched, mesmerized, as her pink tongue swept some of my release off her finger, and she closed her eyes, her brows pinched. I shook my head, utterly embarrassed.

And then, to my awe, she plunged both fingers in her mouth and licked everything off, making my energy pulse through me, crackling and fizzing with emotion.

"May..." I whispered.

She opened her eyes, blushing yet not hiding, and slowly reached under the covers again.

"It tastes good, and it's not food," she said and pressed her lips nervously together. "I think... I might enjoy a snack like this. If you don't mind."

As she licked her fingers again, I shook my head and pressed her closer, not caring that I was spreading my mess—May's *snack*—over both our bodies.

"I'll never deny you anything," I said into her hair. "But what you just did made me want you very much. I have to be inside you."

She hesitated and then turned onto her side, allowing me access to her back. I entered her with utmost care, sliding slowly into her hot, pulsing cunt until she cried out and arched into me, shameless in her pleasure.

"Take what you want from me," I whispered. "It's all yours."

And so she did. Clumsy at first, she soon found a rhythm that pleased us both, and I followed her lead, meeting her hips halfway with my thrusts. Soon, May came with my name on her lips, helped along by my impatient shadow, and I slid out and pressed her back into the mattress, wishing to see her face.

I moved within her, kissing her lips and face, caressing her body, and through my shadow, my happiness poured into her as hers poured into me.

MAY'S EPILOGUE

"This is the place," I said as we stopped in front of the gray, unpleasant edifice of the orphanage. "Virgil, are you sure…"

"Yes," he said, squeezing my hand. "Be brave, my love."

I took a deep breath, which didn't calm me at all, and we slowly ascended the wide steps. In its former life, the building must have been a place where performances were held. It was old, pre-Shift, but much uglier than it must have been, thanks to many repairs using cheap materials. Its façade was faded, and no windows glittered even on the front wall, just the oiled paper stretched between the frames.

I shivered, remembering how cold it always was in winter, how sweltering hot in the summer. This place was hell, and all my demons lived here.

It was a hot day for late April. I didn't remember when my birthday was, but I always remembered my name, so I celebrated on the first of May.

My birthday was tomorrow. This visit was supposed to be a gift to myself.

Only now, I would have rather been anywhere else. If not for Virgil, I would have run and hidden.

"Come," he said, pulling me through the front door. "You said you needed this. To kill your demons."

His eyes turned briefly black, and I shivered, wondering what kind of dark thought made them do that. As the blue glow returned, I gathered my courage and squeezed his hand harder. I led Virgil through my personal hell, passing doorless frames to the rooms where the girls slept, walking deeper into the bowels of the building until I heard music.

"It's practice time," I said, my voice sounding detached and strange. "Gods, Virgil. I just know she will give me that look. She has a way of looking at you that makes you feel like you're nothing. Less than nothing. Ugly, disgusting, unworthy…"

"Then look in my eyes," he said, cupping my face in his palms, his shadow, which was coiled around my heart, purring with emotion. "Look in my eyes and feel what I feel for you."

And I did. A moment later, it poured in. Virgil's love, his adoration, his awe as he looked at my face, tracing my cheeks slowly with his fingers, his glowing eyes searching mine.

I still couldn't believe it sometimes. How very smitten he was with me. How much in love he was. Yet now, his emotions gave me strength, and I squared my shoulders, breathing out with force.

"Let's go," I said, taking his hand.

We walked down the corridor and then down the stairs, to the underground practice room where I sweated so much, cried so much, and suffered for hours a day. Only when I was alone in there, did it bring me joy. When I could dance how I wanted, with no one calling me names and criticizing every line of my body.

I stopped in front of the door, and Virgil laid his palm on my shoulder.

"You are beautiful and brave, my wife," he said, brushing the shell of my ear with his lips. "You're fierce. I believe in you."

I nodded once and opened the door with a bang, making the music inside grow quiet, girls wearing torn practice tutus gasping or smiling when they saw me.

And behind them, standing by the piano... Madame Sundara.

As poised as always, she stood ramrod straight, her lined face severe, eyes cold. Her hair was sleeked back into an even bun, her body cut to perfection despite her age. The ideal I was told to aspire to and always fell short of.

She gave me the look, and for a moment, I felt small. But Virgil's presence at my back and the hopeful, young eyes focused on my face strengthened my resolve.

"I'm taking the girls away," I growled, my voice coming out aggressive.

Inside, I trembled with fear, and in my desperation not to show it, I tapped into my fury.

"Welcome back, May," Madame Sundara said, her withering gaze pressing into my skin like a cold, slimy thing. "I see married life doesn't serve you. You've put on weight, dear. Hope you can lose it fast, or that husband of yours might find a prettier body to hold."

I clenched my jaw, the familiar urge to cower and swear off food forever twisting in my gut. But I couldn't. Twenty pairs of young, hurting eyes were locked on me, and I couldn't fold while they watched.

I grew stronger in my time with Virgil. It had to be enough.

"Your opinion doesn't matter," I gritted out, even though it was a lie. "Girls, I have a home for you. One with whole windows, warm beds, and delicious food. It's in a town ruled by humans, not monsters. You won't have to hide in your beds after dark. You won't have to dance and starve just to keep your little piece of the cold floor. I found you a place where you'll be welcomed, cherished, given fair work, and fed properly."

"How dare you?" Sundara hissed, her scornful gaze turning vicious. "You can't take them away from me! This place is sanctioned by the shifter king."

"He's dealt with," Virgil said, coming closer until the bright light from the practice room revealed his face. The girls gasped, and fear flickered even in the matron's eyes.

"This is my husband," I said proudly, not letting their reactions get to me. "The most powerful being in the world. Even the shifter king fears him. And he will personally guarantee your safety and wellbeing, girls. Come with me."

They hesitated, their eyes going from me to Sundara to Virgil until my husband gently pushed me aside and walked into the room, stopping by the matron's side. She flinched but set her mouth in a line, not stepping away.

With the door cleared, the girls ran out to me with a flurry of greetings and questions. When they were out, I glanced at Virgil, and he motioned for me to go. When I hesitated, the door closed in my face, and I followed the girls to help them pack, anxiety coiling in my stomach.

What was Virgil planning?

When the girls gathered their stuff, and I led them out to the old bus we rented to take us to the portal, Virgil came out, his eyes looking bright, his body crackling with energy.

And without him saying anything, I knew. My heart stuttered, and I stared at my husband, my protector, my lover, who I so often forgot was deadly, lethal, and feared by many.

"What did you do?" I asked, my lips bloodless, my body locked in shock.

"I killed your demons."

We looked at each other until the deep freeze holding me broke, and I fell into his arms. Virgil held me, his shadow soothing me, and while I knew I had a chaos of emotions to untangle later, at that moment, I just felt at peace.

He protected me, he helped me exorcize the evil from my life, and he slayed my demons.

I couldn't have found a better man to love.

VIRGIL'S EPILOGUE

I played the last, gentle notes of the song, gazing up at May. She gave me a nod and a smile, and I slid off the bench, coming over to look at Caspian's sleeping face.

"He really likes your lullabies," May whispered, giving me a radiant smile.

Caspian breathed gently, his small chest moving, his mouth open. He looked like an ordinary human baby, but I noticed the tiniest flickers of his shadow, pressing close to May while he slept, holding on to his mother.

"I'll take him," I whispered back. "And you can dance for me. I'll play."

When she nodded, I gingerly scooped Caspian out of her arms, swathing him in my shadow, holding my son in a warm cocoon of my being. I pressed him close and covered his ears, leaving my hands free to play. After May stretched and warmed up, I played for her, and she danced.

I watched my wife as she turned with grace, leaping high into the air, flying through the ballroom, and my love for her swelled, growing bigger and bigger until all I saw was her and the beautiful child she gave me.

"You are the most beautiful woman in the world," I said when she came closer, her chest rising and falling fast with exertion, a happy smile beaming on her face.

"Even now, after giving birth?" she asked playfully, because she knew what I'd answer.

"Now more than ever. You grow more beautiful every day you stay by my side. With every child you give me, you will become more exquisite."

She kissed me gently, but I captured her lips, and the soft kiss turned into something more languorous, sensual, until May tore away with a groan and gave me a reproachful look.

"You can't do this, you know. Make me all hot when you're holding our son and can't…"

She blushed, still as delightfully innocent as when she married me, and I shook my head, knowing my eyes glowed brighter with humor.

"Can't what, May?"

She threw me a dirty look, glancing around to make sure we were alone, and leaned closer, her face flaming as she whispered, "Fuck me."

It was my turn to feel miffed. When she said dirty words, blushing like that, it undid me in the best of ways.

"I have an idea," I said. "We'll call Agnes, bid her to watch over Caspian, and I can take you to the bedroom and fuck you, as you so aptly put it."

May covered her face with her hands and groaned, but only a moment later, she let her eyes peek out and whispered, "Okay."

Later, when I made love to my beautiful wife, I couldn't help but look with hope and happiness at the eternity that stretched before us. Surrounded by friends, with a prosperous town growing under our care, and wrapped up in each other, we had everything we could ever want. Never before had eternal life seemed so enticing. So absolutely necessary.

Because only eternity would suffice to enjoy my wife and her love to the fullest.

FREE ROMANCE NOVEL

Thank you for reading *Wed to the Lich*! I hope you enjoyed this book. Please, consider leaving me a review on Amazon and Goodreads to help more readers discover this book.

And here's a gift for you! I wrote a paranormal djinn romance that's free to download for everyone. *The Third Wish* is an extra spicy story of Amy, a bubbly artist, and a grumpy djinn who keeps his monstrous nature well hidden... until he meets her.

Download the free romance from my website www.laylafae.com

ARRANGED
MONSTER MATES

If you like the arranged marriage trope, monsters, aliens, and shifters, I invite you to explore the other books in the *Arranged Monster Mates* series. There are more books by me, as well as titles by Eden Ember and Cara Wylde. All books are available on Kindle Unlimited.

Browse the series on Amazon.

BOOKS IN THIS SERIES

Arranged Monster Mates

The Temple, a matchmaking service for monsters, shifters, and aliens, is open for service.

Arranged Monster Mates is a series of novellas written by your favorite paranormal and sci-fi romance authors: Eden Ember, Layla Fae, and Cara Wylde.

Each of these steamy stories has it all: a possessive male, a heroine ready to sacrifice herself to the beast, plenty of spice, and a happily ever after to curl your toes!

Wed To The Orc By Layla Fae

My tiny new wife is a force of chaos bent on turning my life upside down.

I am a researcher. I read books, conduct experiments, and live quietly on the fringes of the orc town. All I want is peace, quiet, and a female to satisfy the wild urges of my orc body so they don't distract me from my work.

Getting a human wife through the Temple seems like a logical solution—until I bring her home and she starts sowing chaos. She moves my books, cuts my herbs to make bouquets, and replaces the blessed silence with laughter and song.

For such a tiny person, she can be very loud. And opinionated.

Worst of all, she does nothing to calm my libido. Instead, she makes my body eager and my mind obsessed. She encroaches on my space, my work, my thoughts, and worst of all, my heart.

I hate being out of control, yet with her, it's all I can be. This cannot go on.

Something has to give.

Wed To The Lionman By Cara Wylde

Betrayed.

The female I'd thought was my mate ran off with someone else in the middle of the night. Now I'm the mock of the pride, the lionman who couldn't rein in his lioness. I don't care what they say. I don't want to control my female, I want her to be with me because I'm her world, like she is mine.

For that to happen, we have to be fated mates. So next time, I won't make the choice. I'll let the Temple choose for me. I send them my blood, and they will find me my perfect match. A female who will never betray me.

Months pass and I hear no word from the Temple. Maybe I'm doomed to be alone. I forget about it and move on with my life.

But one night, while I'm on patrol, I hear a scream. A human female is pursued by three men, and I don't hesitate. I save her honor, her life, and then I look at her...

She is beautiful and pure. I need her to be mine.

Wed To The Bullman By Eden Ember

Minotaurs come to Alia Terra for the sole purpose of finding a mate, starting a family, and growing their presence. They are settling the Taurus Terra territory and filling it with the new half-human, half-minotaur race.

Vozak isn't so sure about the process, but he shows up anyway and puts in for a wife through the Marriage Temple. Since his brother has a human wife, she has him request her sister. Turns out Agnes is a DNA match to him.

It's a rocky start. Agnes comes along with expectations for romance from the old novels she's read and Vozak only knows the minotaur way.

In the process, an enemy comes along and destroys their newfound happiness. Will he be able to save her in time? The fight is on and it's life or death for the new couple.

Wed To Jack Frost By Layla Fae

I just wanted to win a stupid bet – and now I have a wife?!

I made a drunken bet. The Yule was nigh, and Yule's the time when Frost men drink mulled wine and dare each other to stupid stunts. My brother bet I'd be too scared to send a blood sample to the Temple, so of course, I proved him wrong. And before I sobered up enough to withdraw my application…

Ping!

I got matched.

So now I have to go up there and explain to the hapless woman who's apparently my perfect mate that I'm in no hurry to get married. I'm only 54, goddammit! Who even marries so young?

Me, as it turns out. I do. Because the bride that fell in my lap like the most perfect Yule present won't let me leave. She's a harridan and one hell of a bossy shrew who pummels me with cute, lust-provoking insults, and I…

I think I'm in love.

Wed To The Dark Elf By Eden Ember

In a world ruled by monsters and divided by factions, a single DNA match could change the fate of Alia Terra forever. "Wed to the Dark Elf" plunges you into the life-altering journey of Iris Flemming, a human orphan, and Vamen Blak, a formidable dark elf warrior. Thrusted together by tradition but bound by an inexplicable connection, they must navigate political unrest, brewing revolution, and their own conflicting emotions. Will their love be the catalyst for unity or the spark that sets their worlds ablaze? Prepare for a tale of love, war, and transformation that will leave you questioning where your loyalties lie.

Wed To Krampus By Cara Wylde

Is there anyone for me? Or am I meant to live and die alone?

Krampus. It could be my name, or it could be what my species is called. I don't know. During The Shift, something happened, and I lost my memory. I don't know where I come from; all I know is there's no one like me on Alia Terra. I am unique.

Uniquely monstrous. I am hard to look at.

I don't know how old I am, either. Old, for sure, but I feel young. Young enough that I have warmth and love to offer, if only I could find someone to accept me as I am. My only option is the Temple, but even as I let them draw my blood for the DNA test, I have no hope they'll find a match for me.

Against all odds, they do. And she is beautiful, perfect, so sweet, and... horrified when she sees me.

My bride cannot look at my face. How will she see what's in my heart?

BOOKS BY THIS AUTHOR

Jacked: Ghosts Of Halloween

Need a hot read for the spooky season? This is it!

I came here to die. The three masked men won't let me.
It's Halloween. Exactly two years ago, my life shattered, and now I'm back where it happened to finish the job. This house should be empty and abandoned.
It isn't. I meet three masked men who tie me up and do filthy, thrilling things to my body and soul.
Trick or treat?
As it turns out, it's both.

This is a Why Choose MMFM Halloween novella with 18+ content and dark themes. Read responsibly.

Falling For Mr. Hyde

I have one task: assassinate headmaster Hyde. Instead, I surrender to his cruel punishment... and beg for more.

When the Magic Council threatens to deport me, I must agree to their demand I kill Mr. Hyde, Headmaster of Luxior Academy. I am the least qualified shapeshifter for the job. I've never killed so much as a spider.

Hyde is a devious opponent, and he has a powerful, terrifying monster on his side.

Suspicious from the start, they force me to shed my disguise, stripping away my only advantage. We hunt each other, and the deadly dance soon becomes a sensuous play of power and seduction.

As Hyde tries to uncover my secrets, his skillful hands prying at my hidden places, I search for his weak spots. It is my fatal mistake. Instead of weaknesses to exploit, I find a man who is devoted, passionate, and as hard as steel. I don't want to kill him.

No, I'd rather kiss him. Kneel for him. Surrender to anything he - or his monster - commands. I could even be tempted to risk my life to save them.

The stakes are high, and even though I'm in over my head, I need to play dirty to win this game. The problem is, headmaster Hyde wrote its rulebook.

This is a paranormal romance novel with a HEA and adult content. MFM = male, female, monster. It is a standalone. Each book in this monster romance series follows different characters.

Printed in Dunstable, United Kingdom